Sadie had been so happy. They'd both been so happy.

Talking long into the night about all the dreams they had for their child. And each other. They'd been married in a simple ceremony on the beach, when Sadie was seven months pregnant.

"I have every right, Quin. I'm his mother."

Sadie's voice pulled Quin back from the far-too-vivid past. He forced himself to be rational when he felt anything but. In spite of her heinous actions four years ago, he knew that as his son's biological mother, she would have rights. Although he couldn't imagine a court in the land regarding her favourably when she'd walked out of their lives, days after their son was born, without a backward glance.

"What is it you want, Sadie?"

"I want to see my son. I want to be a mother to my son."

Anger bubbled. "You've had four years to be a mother to your son. Why now?"

Irish author **Abby Green** ended a very glamorous career in film and TV—which really consisted of a lot of standing in the rain outside actors' trailers—to pursue her love of romance. After she'd bombarded Harlequin with manuscripts, they kindly accepted one, and an author was born. She lives in Dublin, Ireland, and loves any excuse for distraction. Visit abby-green.com or email abbygreenauthor@gmail.com.

Books by Abby Green

Harlequin Presents

A Ring for the Spaniard's Revenge
His Housekeeper's Twin Baby Confession
Heir for His Empire
"I Do" for Revenge

Passionately Ever After...

The Kiss She Claimed from the Greek

Princess Brides for Royal Brothers

Mistaken as His Royal Bride

Hot Winter Escapes

Claimed by the Crown Prince

Visit the Author Profile page
at Harlequin.com for more titles.

THE HEIR DILEMMA

ABBY GREEN

Harlequin

PRESENTS

ISBN-13: 978-1-335-93939-5

The Heir Dilemma

Copyright © 2024 by Abby Green

Recycling programs for this product may not exist in your area.

For questions and comments about the quality of this book, please contact us at CustomerService@Harlequin.com.

TM and ® are trademarks of Harlequin Enterprises ULC.

 Harlequin Enterprises ULC
22 Adelaide St. West, 41st Floor
Toronto, Ontario M5H 4E3, Canada
www.Harlequin.com

Printed in Lithuania

MIX
Paper | Supporting responsible forestry
FSC® C021394

THE HEIR DILEMMA

I'd like to dedicate this book to my favourite
BBC soap opera, *EastEnders*, and specifically to
Cindy Beale, whose recent return to Albert Square
sparked the idea for this book!

CHAPTER ONE

QUINTANO HOLT SURVEYED the scene before him: a glittering party on the rooftop of one of Manhattan's most iconic hotels. Flaming lanterns and flickering candles bathed some of the most powerful, influential and beautiful people in New York society in a golden glow. Black-and-white-clad waiters moved fluidly through the crowd, offering a choice of beverages and canapés. A full moon hung low in the clear night sky. The air was balmy. All in all, a very exclusive and idyllic scene.

He savoured this moment he had alone to himself, before anyone noticed his arrival. He allowed the sense of satisfaction to settle in his belly. Tonight was the culmination of years of work. He'd floated his tech company on the stock market earlier that day for an astronomical amount of money. This was a celebration of the indelible proof that he could make it on his own. That he hadn't needed his family legacy.

A legacy that he'd sensationally walked away from over five years before, after discovering that his father *wasn't* his biological parent. Some other nameless man had been his father. Maybe the pool boy. Or his Brazilian mother's personal trainer.

Not that the man who had brought him up had tried

very hard to stop him from walking away. He'd taken the news that Quin didn't intend to cash in on his inheritance or take up a role in the family business with a shrug of indifference which had pretty much summed up their relationship.

As for his mother… There were only two people in this world whom he despised and she was one of them. Buried deep inside Quin was the wound of her abandonment, something he'd always blamed himself for. He knew rationally that of course a three-year-old couldn't drive a mother away from her family, but Quin had grown up believing it on a cellular level because of the trauma.

She'd walked out on him and his older brother without a backward glance and she didn't deserve an atom of Quin's energy. He certainly wasn't going to let toxic memories of her infect this moment.

He shut out all unwelcome thoughts and focused on the crowd. He let his gaze wander over the women, each one as stunningly beautiful as the last. Blonde, brunette, jet-black hair, redhead. All poured into dresses that showed off willowy limbs and luscious curves.

All so tempting…and God knew Quin should be tempted. It had been years for him since—

No, not going there. That would be to invite a level of toxicity that went way beyond memories of his mother.

But the problem was that he wasn't tempted. Not even remotely. He looked at these beautiful women and not one caused even a frisson of interest in his blood or his body. He was flatlining.

A sense of desperation climbed upwards. It couldn't be the case that *she'd* ruined him for all women. On top of everything else she'd done. He let his gaze linger on the woman with red hair. She was the one who least resembled *her*. He willed himself to find her attractive, letting his gaze drop over her perfectly toned curves—no doubt honed in one of Manhattan's many sleek gyms.

But that only made him think of another body—equally slim and toned, but from surfing and jogging and walking fast. He'd used to tell her she reminded him of an irrepressible imp, full of kinetic energy. But she'd also been soft in all the right places, and plump in even better places. The way her breast had filled his hand, as if made especially for him… The sharp stab of her nipple… He could still recall how it had felt against his tongue, and the way she'd buck against him, spreading her legs, begging him to—

Quin cursed softly. He was finally feeling aroused and it was thanks to a ghost. Damn her to hell. It was time to move on with his life and if he had to fake it until he felt it then he would do whatever it took.

He was about to take a step towards the party when something made him hesitate. The little hairs went up on the back of his neck. A scent tickled his nostrils. Roses and something sharp. Citrus. Very unique. Only one woman had that scent.

Everything in him tensed. *No.* He would not let her haunt him like this.

Determined to push the past behind him, where it belonged, Quin took a step forward just as a voice said his name from behind him. It was so low that Quin wasn't sure if he'd even heard it.

He stopped, going against every instinct within him

that urged him to keep moving forward. The voice came again, louder this time. Firmer.

'Quin.'

Slowly, Quin turned around, fully expecting to see nothing behind him because his mind was playing tricks. It had to be. Because it couldn't possibly be—

His gaze fell on a woman. *It was her.* The only other person he despised in the world other than his mother. And yet his first instinctive response wasn't disgust, or even rejection, it was something much closer to relief, and an almost overwhelming need to haul her close, touch her…feel for himself how real she was.

No way.

He hated this woman with a passion. It wasn't relief he was feeling. It was pure unadulterated rage and disgust.

And yet the maelstrom inside him wasn't so easily categorised as he took her in…

Slightly above average height. She'd used to love the disparity in their sizes. He was almost a foot taller. She'd run into his arms and wrap her legs around his waist, arms locked around his neck, pressing her mouth to his as if she needed him more than air.

She looked different, though, he vaguely realised through the shock reverberating through his body and brain. Her hair was lighter. Blonde, with reddish streaks. It was down past her shoulders, wavy. Un-styled.

She was pale. Freckles across her cheeks. Aquamarine eyes. Blue and green. Achingly familiar. Long lashes. Straight nose. Wide mouth. Plump lower lip that had made him want to kiss her the first time he'd laid eyes on her.

She wore a plain black evening gown. Strapless.

Showing off a delicate collarbone and slender arms. No blinging jewellery. Minimal make-up. Something about that—about her understated appearance—landed like adrenalin in his gut, waking him out of his shocked trance.

And then he realised it wasn't adrenalin. It was lust.

'Sadie Ryan...' Quin breathed, not quite able to believe he was uttering her name out loud, or that she above all women still had the power to bring his libido back to life after four years.

This was the woman who had betrayed him in the worst way possible—by making him trust her. *Love her.* No, he told himself now. It had never been love. It had been lust. That was all. But the assurance rang hollow, mocking him.

He blinked, hoping that she might disappear. But she didn't. She was all too real.

He said, 'What the hell are you doing here?'

Sadie Ryan looked up at Quin Holt and couldn't quite believe that she was standing here in front of him. And that she was still breathing—that she hadn't fallen, overwhelmed, into a mass of emotion at his feet. Blood was pounding through her body, drowning out the strains of music and the muted chatter of people coming from the party.

He looked as amazing as she remembered... *More.* Short, dark blond hair. Dark eyes. Stubbled jaw. Classically handsome, but with an edge that elevated him to truly gorgeous. Charisma oozed from every pore. As did pure, raw sex appeal.

Past and present seemed to blur into one another as

the memory of seeing him for the first time flashed back into her head. He'd been standing against one of the wooden pillars on the porch that had wrapped around the little beach house in Brazil, drinking from a beer bottle. He'd been wearing nothing but long board shorts. Bare-chested. Utterly gorgeous. And then, as if feeling her gaze on him, he'd looked at her, and she'd felt the electric *zing* from him to her as if they were connected by a wire.

Sadie forced her mind back to the present. She couldn't get lost in memories now. Her mouth was dry from nerves. She tried to swallow, to lick her lips but her tongue and mouth wouldn't function. She'd dreamed of this moment for so long that it didn't feel real.

Emotions churned in her gut and moved upwards, making her chest swell. Finally, *finally* she would get to see—

'I said, what the hell are you doing here?'

Quin's question cut through the emotion. Sadie realised that he looked angry. *No.* Livid. A muscle was popping at his jaw, reminding her of when she'd been in hospital four years ago, in intense pain, and no one had seemed to be listening to her. His jaw had popped like that when he'd been talking to the staff.

She concentrated on the present moment even as the past threatened to drown her in images and memories.

But instead of the rehearsed speech she'd been practising—*I know this must be a shock*—she heard herself blurting out emotionally, 'I'm so happy to see you.'

Quin frowned. Sadie had only barely taken in the dark suit and light blue shirt. The way that his clothes moulded to his tall, powerful body. She'd never seen him so formally dressed. When she'd known him he'd worn a uniform of T-shirts and faded jeans or board shorts, and more often than not he'd spent his time bare-chested. Or naked. Heat flooded her body at that memory.

'You're *"so happy"* to see me?' Quin's voice was incredulous. 'What is this? Some kind of sick joke?'

Sadie shook her head. She cursed her naivety. Of course he wasn't going to be overjoyed to see her. She'd walked out without any explanation. Vanished into thin air. Left him and—

'You were not invited to this party. You should leave.'

The hostility radiating from the man in front of her made Sadie shiver. 'I tried calling you a couple of times recently, but your number must have changed…or maybe you blocked me.'

Quin was silent for a moment, and then he said tautly, 'I had the same number for a year after you left…when you didn't use it, I didn't see any point in keeping it operational. You're not welcome here.'

She said, 'I know I wasn't invited, but I saw in the press that you were due to be here, so I took my chances and they let me in when I said I knew you.'

Quin's dark gaze swept her up and down, nothing warm in it at all. He looked at her and said, 'You *"knew"* me a long time ago.'

Sadie's heart shrank inside her chest. He was looking at her as if she was a stranger and she knew she couldn't blame him.

'Four years isn't that long,' she said weakly, but the lie tasted like acid on her tongue.

The last four years had felt like a lifetime. Each hour crawling past torturously. Each day taking a little bit more of her heart and soul and crushing them to pieces.

Until the glorious moment only a few weeks ago when she'd got the news that she could start living again.

Quin shook his head. 'You have some nerve, showing up like this. What do you want?'

'We need to talk.' Surely he couldn't deny her that?

Quin folded his arms across his chest and Sadie hated how aware of his biceps she was, bulging against the expensive fabric.

'Talk about what? How you disappeared without a trace? Leaving behind only a note with no explanation. How did it go again?'

Quin pretended to think for a second and Sadie wanted to beg him not to say those hateful words that were engraved into her soul. But it was too late, he was biting them out with caustic relish.

'Oh, yes, that was it: *"Please believe me when I say I don't want to leave but I have to…"*'

The fact that he'd omitted part of the note was small comfort. Maybe he didn't want to remember the bit where she'd said, 'I love you.' Or the other part, which was why she was here…

'Quin.' She tried to appeal to the side of him that didn't want to vaporise her on the spot. 'We need to talk. We need to talk about—'

'We have nothing to talk about,' he cut her off brutally. 'You need to turn around and leave right now, or I'll have you thrown out.'

Panic clutched at Sadie's gut. He couldn't do this. But her limbs were turning to jelly at the thought that he might very well have her unceremoniously thrown out onto the streets, that she might not get to see—

She forced air to her panicking brain. She had to be rational and remember she had rights.

She forced herself to stand tall in the face of his white-hot anger and clear rejection of her presence. 'I'm not going anywhere, Quin. I've come here because I want to see my son. *Our* son, Quin. I want to see Sol.'

CHAPTER TWO

QUIN STILL COULDN'T believe that Sadie was standing before him. And uttering his son's name out loud. It was blasphemy, coming from her. The woman who had walked out on her days-old baby. Their son. *No.* His son. She'd given up her rights to be his mother the day she'd turned her back on him with such callous disregard.

He of all people should have realised it might happen. After all it had happened to him. In his world mothers wreaked nothing but havoc.

The need to protect his son from this woman and whatever she wanted was overwhelming. He said, 'How dare you even mention his name? You have no right.'

She went even paler in the dim light. Eyes wide. The colour of the ocean. He'd used to drown in her eyes. He'd fought it for a long time when they'd first met, having never really trusted anyone after his mother had walked out on him at such a young age. But day by day he'd fallen deeper and deeper under this woman's spell, until one day he'd woken up and realised that he'd die for her. She had become his world.

That was when she'd told him she was pregnant, looking as shocked as he'd felt. But then there had been an overwhelming surge of joy and hope. He was being given a chance to do things differently...to change the script. He'd naively looked forward to witnessing a mother who loved her child enough to stay. He'd relished the opportunity to show his child love and support. Not the indifference he'd experienced from his father.

Quin had grown up with unbelievable privilege—anything money could buy, but nothing of real value. He'd learnt about that value by carving out his own path, and the thought of being able to pass that on to his child had been incredibly cathartic.

Sadie had been so happy—they'd both been so happy. Talking long into the night about all the dreams they had for their child. And each other. They'd been married in a simple ceremony on the beach, when Sadie was seven months pregnant...

'I have every right, Quin. I'm his mother.'

Sadie's voice pulled Quin back from the far too vivid past. He forced himself to be rational when he felt anything but. In spite of her heinous actions four years ago, he knew that as his son's biological mother, she did have rights. Although he couldn't imagine a court in the land regarding her favourably when she'd walked out of their lives, days after their son was born, without a backward glance.

'What is it you want, Sadie?'

'I want to see my son. I want to be a mother to my son.'

Anger bubbled. 'You've had four years to be a mother to your son. Why now?'

Something occurred to him then, and it made his guts curdle with disgust. At one time he'd believed he'd

known this woman as well as himself, but he'd been utterly naive.

She was opening her mouth, but he uncrossed his
arms and held up a hand. 'No need to say a thing. Your
timing says it all.'

'My timing?'

She looked genuinely nonplussed. Quin might have
laughed if he'd felt remotely like it. Her acting skills really were superb. Another thing he'd never given her
credit for, because he'd trusted her.

'You expect me to believe it's a coincidence that you
appear back in my life on the day that I float my company on the stock market and it makes millions?'

Well, actually billions, but Quin wasn't going to be
pedantic.

She shook her head, 'No, that's not it at all.' She
blushed. 'I'd been following you in the news, to try and
figure out the best way to contact you, and I read about
your success…but I'm not interested in that side of it. I
mean…' She stopped and then said huskily, 'I am interested in the fact that you've achieved everything you'd
set out to achieve when I first met you. It's amazing,
Quin, you must be so proud.'

His chest squeezed at the way she said his name
like that, catching him unawares. He'd confided in this
woman…all his hopes and dreams. Ambitions. He'd
opened up to her in a way he'd never done with anyone
else—not even his older brother—helplessly seduced by
her open and loving nature, never thinking for a second
that she would be the one to rip his world apart.

More fool him. At one time he'd imagined sharing this
moment with her, but now the triumph felt somehow…

tainted. As if trusting her with those nascent dreams was now invalidating everything.

The past was all around him, closing in, whispering in his ear and sending a kaleidoscope of incendiary images into his brain. He forced ice into his blood, but the throb of awareness was almost impossible to quench. It always had been. From the moment he'd laid eyes on this woman he'd wanted her with a primal need that he'd never felt before. He needed to push her back.

'You say you're only here to see your son? In that case I'll give you my solicitor's details and you can contact me through the appropriate legal channels.'

Sadie could feel her blood drain south, and for a second she felt dizzy. She must have swayed slightly or something, because Quin said, 'Are you okay?'

But he didn't sound concerned—he sounded irritated. Sadie nodded. She wasn't going to wilt at his feet like some sort of waif. Even if it had been hours since she'd eaten; she'd been too nervous. And she hadn't slept much since she'd arrived in New York from England the day before.

'I'm fine.' She needed to be strong, to appeal to Quin. 'Look, I don't have the kind of funds required to hire a solicitor to enter into legal proceedings to gain access to my son. I just want to see my son and spend some time with him.'

Quin shot back without hesitation, 'And then what? Disappear again without a trace? One advantage of leaving when you did the last time was that he was only a few days old. He's four now, and he has a mind like a steel trap. He notices everything and everyone.'

Emotion bubbled up at how he described Sol, stinging Sadie's eyes before she could stop it. Her knowledge of her son had been confined to very grainy paparazzi photos of Quin and Sol taken over the years, compounding her pain and loneliness at having left them.

When it had become apparent that Quintano Holt, son of legendary billionaire and industry titan Robert Holt, was a single father, the social columns had gone into a frenzy, speculating about where Quin had been for the past few years and how he'd become a single father.

Sadie hadn't known about Quin's own father—or, apparently, according to the gossip sites, the man who was *not* his biological father. She hadn't known that he had an older brother, or that he'd come from an incredibly privileged background, born into one of America's founding families.

Quin had never spoken much about his life before he'd met Sadie during the year they'd been together, only telling her that he wasn't close to his family. She'd sensed his reticence to talk about it and so she hadn't pushed. After all, she'd only known the full extent of her own past for a couple of days when she'd first met him...

But now was not the time to get into all of that. They had bigger issues. She forced the emotion down and said, 'I'm not going anywhere. Not again. I'm here to stay. I'm here to be a mother to Sol.'

Even though the thought terrified her. She'd been his mother for mere days before she'd known she had no choice but to leave, for Quin and Sol's safety.

Quin made a snorting sound. 'Based on previous behaviour, I'd say there are two chances of you sticking around: slim and none.'

Sadie needed to try and convince him somehow, and the only thing she could convince him with was the truth—but she could already imagine Quin laughing his head off. Disbelieving her. Even though it would be easy to prove.

She pleaded, 'Give me a chance to explain why I left, Quin—please. If you'd just—'

But he held up his hand and stopped her words. She watched him take a small phone out of an inner jacket pocket and press a button, then hold it up to his ear. He turned away slightly, and even that attempt to hide himself from her was wounding. When they'd been together he'd never hidden from her.

Except that wasn't true. Quin Holt *had* hidden a huge amount from her—not least his significant family history. In the year that she'd known him she'd assumed that he was little more than a surfer boy and a tech nerd, travelling and working remotely because he had no ties, or none that he cared much about.

Not that Sadie could claim any moral high ground after what she'd done and what she'd hidden about herself. But right now she needed to gain his trust, not alienate him.

She realised he was talking Portuguese, specifically Brazilian Portuguese. He sounded a lot more fluent than he'd been when they'd been living in a small surfing beach town to the east of Sao Paulo in Brazil. Evidently they'd both had their reasons for being in such a place, where one could get lost. Except she'd forgotten her reasons for being there thanks to a head injury sustained while surfing, just two days after she'd first laid eyes on him. He'd been the one who had pulled her out of the water and who had saved her life.

For almost the entire year she'd been with Quin, in a whirlwind, passionate and life-changing relationship, she hadn't remembered a thing about who she really was. She'd felt incredibly vulnerable after the accident, but he'd won her trust by taking care of her and expecting nothing in return. And then, over the days and weeks that had followed, their building attraction had finally become too powerful to ignore and they'd become lovers, inseparable.

Somehow, the fact that she couldn't remember who she was, or anything of her past, had almost faded into the background. They'd been so caught up in each other, in a dreamlike bubble. It had been easy to forget that Quin must have had a past too. He'd become her anchor. And the love of her life.

She'd only regained her memory after the birth of Sol. And that had led to her fateful exodus—the hardest thing she'd ever had to do in her life. And the most painful.

Quin had terminated his phone conversation now and was looking at her. Sadie tried again, 'Please, Quin—'

But he cut her off. 'I don't have time now to hear whatever story you've concocted to explain how you could have walked away from your own baby without a backward glance. I'm returning to Brazil.'

She hadn't walked away without a backward glance. Far from it. Every day since then had been an absolute torture. The only thing that had got her through those endless days had been the knowledge that she'd done what she'd done to keep Quin and Sol safe at all costs. And the cost had been huge. But worth it. Even now, in the face of Quin's hostility and anger. Even if he never forgave her.

The need to defend herself mixed with panic at the thought that Quin was going to just walk away. She focused on what he'd said.

'Brazil? What's in Brazil?'

'I live in Sao Paulo with Sol.'

Sadie's heart clenched. That was where he'd been born.

'Sol is there now?'

She wanted to ask him how he could leave their son behind, thousands of miles away, but she bit her lip. She didn't really have that right.

'Yes, he's there. With his very much adored and capable nanny, who has been with us since you left.'

Another poison dart to Sadie's heart.

Quin continued, 'I haven't even been gone twenty-four hours. I was planning on staying in Manhattan overnight and returning in the morning, but I've decided to leave now.'

Sadie deflated. There was no way she could afford to travel to Sao Paulo and follow Quin. It had taken all her paltry finances to come to New York at short notice when she'd read that he would be here for the stock market flotation.

'Quin, I—'

'Look. I'm going to give you one chance.' His jaw was tight. 'Not that you deserve it. But, as much as I hate to admit it, you do have some rights, and when this comes to court—as it inevitably will—I don't want you to have any reason to lay accusations at my door that I didn't give you an opportunity to see my son. I won't take any risks when it comes to Sol and ensuring I remain his primary custodial parent, so if that means allowing you some initial access then I'll do it.'

Sadie surmised that the brief phone conversation must have been with his legal team. They would have advised him to tread carefully. She didn't much care, because all she felt was huge relief. 'I… That's amazing, thank you.'

But then she remembered her limitations, and her insides plummeted again. 'It's not that I wouldn't jump at the opportunity right now, but the truth is that I can't afford to go to Brazil at such short notice…'

She heard herself and winced. She sounded as if she was making excuses. No doubt Quin would jump on this to cast her off.

She waited for him to smirk and tell her, *Tough.*

But he didn't smirk. He just looked at her with unnerving intensity. Then he said, 'I will have to take your word for it when it comes to your means—after all who knows what you've been up to for the last four years? Are you married? Do you have more children?'

Sadie felt a bubble of hysteria rise up at the notion. She pushed it down and shook her head. 'No, nothing like that. Of course not.' She thought of something and asked, 'Do you? Have a partner?'

She hadn't seen pictures of him with anyone, but then he'd never been showy…

His mouth tightened, but he said eventually, 'Not that it's any of your business, but no, I'm not with anyone right now.'

But he had been? That was what he was implying. Sadie's insides twisted with something dark. Jealousy.

ABBY GREEN   25

A jealousy she had no right to feel. And yet she heard herself say, 'We *are* still married.'

Quin let out a curt laugh. 'Hardly. That beach wedding was ceremonial only. We never signed anything.'

Sadie flushed. Of course. They'd been due to have a proper, legal ceremony after Sol's birth...but then her world had been turned upside down with the return of her memory.

'Of course... I know that,' she said now, feeling gauche and naive.

She'd always believed that beautiful ceremony on the beach had been more binding than anything in a church or a register office. Clearly he hadn't. But at the time it had felt so real. The way he'd looked at her...as if she was the only thing in the world.

She hid her hands behind her back and removed the ring he'd proposed to her with—an emerald and sapphire ring that had become her single most treasured item, along with a picture she'd taken of Quin holding newborn Sol before she'd left. The thought of Quin seeing her still wearing the ring now made her skin go clammy with panic. As did the thought of him seeing the short unvarnished nails and careworn skin of her hands. They were evidence of her constant moving around and the only work that had been available to her, which had inevitably been menial and backbreaking.

'I can explain what I've been doing, if you'll let me.'

Except what if she told him and he thought it was so outlandish and unbelievable that he cast her out of his and Sol's lives for good? Her mind raced, thinking of that scenario—by the time she'd worked to make enough money to try and see Sol again he'd be a teenager.

She realised that she couldn't explain here, like this, with them facing each other like bitter adversaries. She blurted out, before Quin could answer, 'Actually, maybe now isn't such a good time.'

He arched a brow. 'You need more time to come up with the right story?'

Sadie swallowed. 'It's not like that…it's just a lot to explain…'

He glanced at his watch. 'I don't have time for this. I've instructed my plane to be ready to leave within the hour. You can come with me.'

Sadie stopped breathing for a second. He was going to take her with him? She was afraid she'd misheard him.

But then he asked impatiently, 'Where are you staying?'

Sadie quickly gave the address of the travellers' hostel near Central Station, afraid he might change his mind. Quin's eyes widened marginally at the mention of the hostel, and now that she knew of his background she could well imagine why.

He said briskly, 'I'll have someone go and pick up your things. They can meet us at the plane.'

Sadie thought of the mess she'd left behind as she'd hurriedly changed into this dress, which she'd bought in a discount store earlier that day. 'Is that really necessary? I can rush back now and pack…'

But he shook his head, already taking out his phone again, giving instructions.

This new businesslike version of Quin was a revelation to her. When she'd known him he'd been the quintessential surfer traveller. He'd also been a tech nerd, spending hours a day on his laptop, not issuing instructions like this.

But then that memory returned of when they'd gone to the hospital in Sao Paulo, for her to have Sol. For the first time she'd seen Quin in authoritative mode, and the way the doctors and nurses had meekly acquiesced to his instructions, as if sensing his innate authority. No wonder. He'd been oozing generations of privilege and entitlement.

She hadn't taken too much notice at the time, because she'd been in the middle of intense labour pains, but now it clicked into place like a missing jigsaw piece. As did the fact that he'd managed to get her into a private birthing suite at the hospital. At the time she'd wondered only vaguely how they could afford it...

She felt naive now. For not questioning him about his past more. For trusting him so blindly.

He handed her the phone. 'Tell Martha what she needs to know to pack your things.'

Sadie took the phone and turned away from Quin, not wanting him to hear her apologising for the state of the room before telling the perfectly polite woman on the other end where her things were. She'd always been messy, in contrast to Quin's almost fanatical tidiness.

She turned around again and handed back the phone. 'Thank you. I really appreciate you taking me with you.'

'I'm not doing it for your benefit, believe me. My driver is waiting.'

Quin put out a hand for Sadie to precede him out of the area leading into the party. She noted that he was careful not to touch her. She was grateful, even as she

ached for his touch. She didn't need him seeing how at-
tuned to him she still was after all this time.

In the back of the chauffeur-driven car, the air between
them was frigid. Quin looked out of the opposite window, brooding. He must be irritated that she'd disrupted
his evening. Sadie sat still, afraid that if she moved even
an inch Quin would change his mind and throw her out
onto the road.

But the car sped on, through the streets and off the island of Manhattan to a private airfield, where a woman
in a smart trouser suit was waiting with Sadie's small
wheelie case, which she'd been dragging around with her
for years now. At that moment Sadie wanted to throw it
into the nearest bin, she was so heartily sick of it and its
reminders of what she'd endured.

But it would have one last journey to make—because
she wasn't leaving her son's side ever again, no matter
how she did it. Even if she had to camp outside Quin's
home.

And at least she didn't have to worry about how to
get there.

The fact that they were stepping onto a sleek black
private jet was almost negligible to Sadie, she was so
eager to get to her son. But once on board she couldn't
help but notice the plush opulence. The softest carpet,
and cream leather seats with gold trim. Quin was walking down the plane to some seats near the back. Not sure
what to do, Sadie just followed him.

He sat down and looked at her. He waved a hand towards the other seats. 'Make yourself comfortable. It's
a long flight—between nine and ten hours. We'll arrive

in the morning. Sao Paulo is an hour ahead of our current time.'

Sadie became very aware of her dress. She gestured to
herself. 'I'll change, then, into something more practical.'

Quin gestured behind him to a door. 'The bedroom
and bathroom are in there. Be my guest.'

Sadie had disappeared into the bedroom with the small
case that seemed to be her only possession. Quin was so
tense he wondered if he hadn't burst a few blood vessels.
Her scent lingered in the air, taunting him. He cursed and
forced himself to relax as the crew prepared for take-off.

He still couldn't quite believe that she had appeared
in front of him within the last hour, as if conjured out
of his imagination. But the response in his body was an
unwelcome reminder that she was all too real. His blood
was still hot. Sizzling. His muscles were aching from the
control it had taken for him not to reach out and touch
her... See if she was real. See if her skin still felt as soft.
Her hair as silky.

He'd been aware of every minute move she'd made
in the back of the car, barely breathing in case her scent
went too deep inside him.

He wondered if he was crazy to be bringing her with
him. But his legal counsel, whom he'd spoken to on the
phone, had told him to find out what she wanted. They'd
advised telling her to contact them through the proper
channels. They hadn't said to keep her close at all costs.
That was his own decision. An instinct to keep an eye
on her... In case she disappeared again?

No, he told himself. It was a practical move to make

sure he knew what she was up to. If she was with him, she couldn't take him by surprise again.

He scowled at himself. She'd disappeared once before, and he had no doubt she would do it again. He just had to figure out what it was she was after. Because she might deny that timing had anything to do with it, but it was almost laughable that she'd chosen this exact moment to reappear.

He'd been independently wealthy for the last few years, once his startup had gained attention and traction, but the stock market flotation had put it and him onto another level. She'd obviously been biding her time. She'd known based on what he'd told her back then that this might happen one day. She was the one who had first encouraged him and told him it was a great idea.

Maybe—the thought occurred to him—she was going to try and claim some kind of ownership of the company? Make a case for him owing her something of the profits?

At that moment the door opened behind him and he tensed all over again as her scent preceded her. She walked past him and he noticed that she'd replaced the dress with faded jeans and soft pink short-sleeved top. She'd pulled her hair back into a messy knot. But he couldn't look away from where the material of her jeans lovingly cupped her heart-shaped backside. As pert and plump as he remembered. Small waist. Narrow torso. Firm breasts.

One of his last memories of her was when she'd been breastfeeding Sol in their bed, after they'd returned to Sao Sebastiao on the coast. She'd been pale. Distracted. He'd put it down to the stress of trying to get the baby to feed properly. He'd been fractious. As if he'd sensed that something was wrong... But how could he have known that his mother would walk out and leave him just a couple of days later?

Clearly she'd known something then too... After Sol was born she'd changed, become withdrawn, hadn't been able to meet his eye. Again, he'd assumed it was just to be expected after something as monumental as giving birth.

She turned around now, and Quin forced his gaze up and tried not to let those huge green-blue eyes unsettle him. Except he had to concede that every time his son looked at him with those exact same eyes he was reminded of his errant mother.

No wonder Quin hadn't felt remotely like pursuing another woman in the meantime. Sadie had been like a resident ghost. But she wasn't a ghost any more.

She said, 'I...ah...just wanted to say thank you... again.'

From behind her, Quin saw one of the staff send him a signal and he welcomed it. He said, 'We're about to take off. You should take a seat and buckle in.'

'Of course, yes.'

She looked around and chose a seat that put her facing away from Quin. That made him feel irritable—and then *that* made him feel even more irritable.

He buckled his own belt and focused on the plane taxiing and taking off into the night sky over New York—and *not* on the woman who was sitting just feet away. The same woman who had built him up only to tear him down and remind him that he'd been an utter idiot to believe in love or that trust could ever exist.

There were only two things he trusted in this world now: himself and his son. The sooner he knew what Sadie Ryan was up to, the sooner he could put her at a safe distance again.

CHAPTER THREE

SAO PAULO WAS full of tall, soaring buildings as far as the eye could see. They hadn't driven into the city itself. They were somewhere on the outskirts, on wide, leafy streets. As they'd stepped out of the plane a short while before, the early-morning sun had made the nearby city glimmer in the golden light.

A new day, a new dawn. Sadie had taken it as a sign of better days to come and clung on to that now.

Surely now she could start to rebuild her life? Make amends for what she'd had to do? Be a mother to her son…?

'You didn't sleep much on the plane. You could have gone into the bedroom.'

Sadie tensed at virtually the first words Quin had uttered since they'd taken off from New York. He'd noticed her restlessness. She'd been doing her best to try and ignore him and her awareness of him. He'd changed on the plane at some point—into khaki trousers and a short-sleeved white polo shirt. He looked dark and suave and ridiculously sexy, his clothes doing little to hide the powerful body underneath.

Sadie felt self-conscious. She knew she must look tired. And wan. A far cry from the golden tan she'd had

the last time she'd known Quin…golden from practically living on the beach. They'd spent more time in the
water than on land.

'I'm fine,' she said now. 'I'm not a great sleeper at the
best of times.'

Although she knew that the truth of her restlessness
had more to with Quin's proximity and the impending
reunion with her son than with anything else.

'You slept fine when—' Quin stopped abruptly.

Sadie's heart thumped. 'When we were together?'

He didn't answer. He might want to pretend it hadn't
happened…their relationship. But it had. They had a little boy as proof that once he'd loved her.

She said, 'I did sleep well with you.'

She blushed. When they'd actually slept. Usually
around dawn, after spending hours exploring each other
with a thoroughness that had left her wrung out and
destroyed by pleasure. But it had been a beautiful de-
struction.

She'd felt so safe with Quin, in his arms. It had been a
completely instinctive sense of well-being, as if as long
as she was with him everything would be okay. No wonder her mind had been blank of the horrors—

'You used to have nightmares.'

Except for those. Her subconscious had provided images at night that she hadn't been able to understand,
and it had only been when her memory returned that
she'd realised the nightmares were based on reality. Her
memory taunting her.

'I don't get them any more.'

Her reality had been enough of a nightmare for the last
four years. Now her sleep was broken up with wonder-

ing if and how she'd get to see her son. And Quin. And now here she was. Moments away from meeting her son.

'Does he ever ask about me?' Sadie blurted out before she could stop herself.

Quin shot her a glance. 'He's only just started to recently. Since realising that he's the only one of his friends who doesn't have a mother.'

Sadie felt a little sick. 'What have you told him?'

'That you had to go away.'

Just that. So stark. No mention of the anguish and pain it had caused her to leave.

The car was slowing to a stop outside relatively inconspicuous-looking gates with lush greenery screening anything behind them from the road.

But Sadie could see the gates were tall and fortified. She also noticed the discreet security men just inside, as the gates swung open as if by magic to admit them.

The car proceeded up a long driveway, bordered on each side by thick vegetation, until suddenly they emerged into a vast open courtyard in front of a modern structure on different levels that somehow managed to blend in with the vegetation around it, as if it had been there for hundreds of years.

Lots of clean lines and glass—more glass than she'd ever seen on a building.

The car pulled to a stop, and before Sadie could prepare herself, the front door of the house opened and a blur of energy ran down the steps towards the car. Quin was out of the car, leaving the door open, and bending down with arms outstretched, ready to welcome his son.

His son. Their son. Her baby boy.

Sadie couldn't breathe. She couldn't move. She was frozen as she watched this tableau from inside the car.

Quin swung Sol up into his arms and she heard Sol saying ecstatically, 'Papa, you're home already! Lena said you wouldn't be back till later!'

'I wanted to surprise you.'

Shakily, Sadie somehow managed to get out of the car. The driver had opened her door. She stood up and could feel the sun beating down on her head. She looked across the roof of the car at her son and couldn't believe it. He was leaning back in Quin's arms now, grinning. He was all at once familiar and totally strange to her. Even though she could see he took after her with his strawberry blond colouring. He had her eyes. Light green-blue. But he had his father's darker-toned skin. Golden. He had freckles. And an impish smile.

As if feeling her avid gaze on him he turned his head and looked at her. He said, very baldly, 'Who are you?'

Who was she? She was a stranger. She was this little boy's mother. She was lost. She was drowning in a sea of emotions.

She opened her mouth. 'I—'

'She's a friend from work. She's come to help me with a project,' Quin interjected smoothly.

Sol seemed to take this with total equanimity. 'What's her name, Papa?'

Sadie didn't look at Quin. She could hardly take her eyes off her son.

Quin said, 'Her name is Sadie.'

Sol repeated it. 'Sadie… I don't know anyone with that name. That's cool.'

The little boy scrambled down out of Quin's arms

and came to stand in front of Sadie. She wasn't sure how she was still standing when she couldn't feel her legs any more.

Sol looked up at her. She noticed he was wearing a T-shirt with a school logo and matching shorts. Scuffed sneakers. There was a scab on his knee. He was clearly active.

He said, 'Hey, do you want to see my bedroom? It's pretty cool. I've got posters of my favourite football players.'

Somehow Sadie found her voice through the blood rushing to her head at the enormity of this moment. 'You like football?'

He nodded. 'It's the best ever. When I get older I'm going to play for Sao Paulo.'

'You are? That's—'

'Come on, Sol, time to go to school. You'll see Sadie later.'

His eyes widened, mirror images of his mother's. 'You're *staying* here?'

Sadie dragged her gaze from her son to look at Quin helplessly. She hadn't even thought about what would happen when she got here. She had no money to pay for accommodation.

His expression was unreadable, and he just said to his son, 'Perhaps.'

And then an older woman appeared behind Quin, middle-aged, with a kind face and a shrewd gaze that went from Sol to Sadie.

Quin said, 'This is Madalena. Sol's nanny and my saviour.'

Sadie smiled weakly at the woman as Sol piped up with, 'But we call her Lena, 'cos it's shorter.'

Madalena came and shook Sadie's hand, smiling warmly. 'Welcome to Sao Paulo. Excuse us, but it's time for this young man to get to school.'

She took his hand and they walked away, Sol jumping beside the woman, unable to control his energy. When they'd got into a small car and driven down the driveway Sadie almost sagged back against the bigger car, adrenalin draining down through her body. Quin was standing to the side, watching her carefully, hands in his pockets.

She shook her head. 'I don't know…what to say. He's beautiful…more beautiful than I could have imagined.'

'Yes, he is. He's turned out to be a happy, secure little boy…in spite of everything.'

Sadie absorbed the dig. She suddenly felt exhausted, the culmination of the last few days catching up with her.

'You look washed out.'

'Thanks,' Sadie said dryly.

'Come on, we'll get something to eat and then I'll show you where you can stay.'

'I am staying here?'

He looked at her. 'If you're sticking to your story of not having any money then I'm assuming you'll need a place to stay?'

There was no point trying to defend herself, so Sadie just said simply, 'I would appreciate that, yes.'

She followed Quin into the vast modern structure, eyes widening as she took in the open, airy spaces. Wood finishes softened the concrete walls and floors. Abstract art added splashes of colour, as did huge rugs with local designs. She caught glimpses of lush foliage all around them through the windows and a pristine green lawn in the distance.

Quin pointed out the dining room beside a massive open-plan kitchen where a man was working at the cooker. He greeted Quin with a smile and they exchanged a few words.

Quin turned to Sadie. 'This is Roberto, Madalena's husband. He's our chef. They both live just next door, through an adjoining garden.'

Sadie smiled shyly. 'Nice to meet you, Roberto.'

She'd spent so much time in the intervening years avoiding making much contact with people that it felt strange to be able to do this. The man was like his wife, his gaze friendly, but also shrewd. Sadie had the feeling it wouldn't take much for them to put two and two together.

Quin was striding onwards. Sadie had to hurry to keep up. Clearly he wasn't giving her this tour out of a sense of solicitousness. There was a sitting room off that area, and another one that could be closed off with sliding doors. There was a gym, and a vast home office.

Sadie asked, 'You work from home?'

'Sometimes, but I have an office in Sao Paulo. I employ close to a hundred people now and we're growing all the time.'

'That's really...cool,' she finished a little lamely, borrowing the word that Sol seemed to like using.

Quin was opening a massive sliding door that led off the open-plan space of the living area out to the garden. Sadie followed him. It was so tranquil. The only sounds were birds calling and the muted hiss of water sprinklers.

There were portable goal posts set up—presumably for Sol to play football.

As she followed him down the lawn on strategically placed flagstones Quin said, 'The entire property is completely self-sustaining. We use solar panels and we have a well. We grow as much of our own produce as we can, and our housekeeper supplies a local homeless charity with the excess.'

Sadie's heart squeezed. They'd once talked for hours about how they would live sustainably, careful to consider the life of their unborn child. 'That's impressive.'

Quin glanced back at her. 'Sol is obsessed with the planet and environment. His school is big into teaching them about sustainability.'

'Isn't four a little young for school?'

'It's a preschool class at the International School, until he's six. Then he'll be entering into the main curriculum.'

'Oh.' Sadie knew that Quin would not appreciate her opinion on how to school their child. Not after abandoning him.

Quin was disappearing down a path between the trees now, and Sadie followed him into a lush, quiet space where a separate building stood. It was in the same vein as the main house but smaller—lots of glass and wood and concrete, all on one level—yet it still managed to blend in with the background.

Quin said, 'This is our guest house. You can stay here.'

So she wasn't to be allowed in the familial space. Silly to feel hurt. But it was a reminder that when her memory had returned she'd realised just how alone she'd been all her life—first because of her parents' tragic premature deaths and then through years of a failed adoption and fostering.

No wonder she'd cleaved to Quin with such passion and blind trust. He'd been the first person to give her any sense of total security and *love*. A sense of home.

After the surfing accident Quin had offered to let her stay with him—the relative stranger who had saved her life. It had been nuts to say yes, but she'd known on some deep level that she could trust him.

Ostensibly it had been for practical reasons—the hospital had said they weren't going to release Sadie after the head trauma she'd suffered—and also because she'd lost her memory—unless she could be observed and cared for. There had been no friends rushing forward to offer to take care of her. Her mobile phone had been lost or stolen in the aftermath of the accident. She'd been on her own and vulnerable.

But by the time Sadie had fully recovered, there had been no question of her moving out. By then, she and Quin had embarked on a passionate love affair. All-consuming and life-changing.

She forced down the echoes of the past and moved forward to take in the sizeable property, hoping that her emotions wouldn't show on her face. 'This is more than generous, Quin.'

He was moving to the side of the property and Sadie followed him, even though it didn't seem as if he much cared if she did.

He stood at a break in the trees and pointed. 'The pool is through there, and the pool house is fully stocked with swimwear and robes, if you want to swim.'

Just looking at the pool made Sadie feel dusty and

grimy. It was deliciously inviting, barely a ripple on the green-blue water as it glistened under the sun.

Quin was already moving back to the house, going up a couple of steps, opening the front door. He stood aside to let her pass him and his scent—hints of sea and leather and earth—made her want to close her eyes to breathe him in fully. She kept them wide open and held her breath.

This building was like a micro version of the main house—open spaces, flowing rooms. A massive bedroom suite with dressing room and bathroom. The bathroom had a shower area that was open to the elements, and a colourful bird flew past as Sadie looked up. It was whimsical and romantic.

She quickly diverted her attention back to Quin's whistlestop tour to crush such rogue notions.

There was a fully stocked kitchen, and a living area that had a luxurious L- shaped couch and a massive TV, even a separate dining area. There was a utility room— the height of luxury to Sadie, who had been pretty much living out of her case and washing her clothes in laundromats for four years.

Again, there were colourful rugs and art to soften the stark modern lines. Sadie liked the style, she found it soothing.

Quin was talking. 'We have a housekeeper too—Sara. She's probably in town, shopping for supplies. She'll unpack your things when she returns.'

Sadie thought of her paltry belongings and said quickly, 'There's no need for that. I'll come and get my case.'

Quin shrugged. 'Suit yourself.' He glanced at his

watch. 'We'll have something to eat and then I have to go into the office.'

He led the way back up to the main house through the garden, and Sadie once again hurried after him to keep up. A vivid memory assailed her of running to catch up with Quin on the beach in Sao Sebastiao, and how she'd jumped onto his back. He'd caught her legs under her knees. She'd wrapped her arms around his neck and kissed him, tasting the salt of the sea on his skin.

She stumbled on one of the flagstones, and was pitching forward with a small cry when Quin turned around and caught her.

She fell against him with a small *oof*.

An immediate wave of heat flushed through her entire body, bringing cells alive that had lain dormant for four years. Electricity hummed along her skin, raising the small hairs. Lust, immediate and raw, pooled in her belly.

She looked up, off-balance and helpless against the storm raging inside her at being so close to him. His eyes were unreadable, though. Two pools of dark obsidian. No chink of light. No forgiveness. Jaw tight. Nostrils flaring.

Before she knew what was happening Quin was putting her away from him with two strong hands on her arms and letting her go. Practically pushing her away. Showing his distaste for having any part of them touching.

Her face flamed. 'I'm sorry. I wasn't watching where I was going.'

He was already turning around and striding forward, saying, 'It's nothing. Don't worry about it.'

Sadie followed, and wondered if this man would ever

look at her again the way he had on that beautiful day on the beach when they'd been married by a humanist celebrant. Joined by love and the baby growing in her belly. He'd looked at her as if she was the only precious thing in the world. She'd felt so loved…treasured. And she knew that she'd been looking at him the same way because he had been her world.

Still was.

No matter how she might wish otherwise, she'd never stopped loving him. How could she? He was the father of her child. He'd been her first lover.

It had been so perfect…and yet it had dissolved so easily. Yes, her transgression had been huge. Perhaps unforgivable, maybe even when he knew her reasons why.

All she could hope for was that when the dust had settled, and when they'd established an acceptable routine in which she could be part of her son's life on a permanent basis, one day Quin might not look at her with such abject loathing…

Quin picked up Sol from school that day, to give Lena a break, and all Sol could talk about on the drive back to the house was *Sadie*. It was unusual. Sol liked people, and wasn't shy, but he didn't usually fixate on someone like this. Clearly he'd sensed something about her.

The fact that when he'd stood in front of his mother earlier you'd have had to be blind not to have noticed the resemblance between them.

It had knocked the air out of Quin's lungs and then made his chest squeeze tight. He'd seen the narrow-eyed look in Lena's eye. Nothing got past that woman. Or Roberto. But they hadn't said anything. Yet.

Sol jumped out of the car now, when Quin came to a halt in the main courtyard, and ran into the house. Quin followed, feeling tense. Sol was in the kitchen, helping himself to the healthy snacks Roberto had left out for him—a little post-school ritual. Not for the first time Quin was endlessly grateful that he had such good support around him. Being a single parent was probably the hardest thing he'd ever done. And it had only compounded his anger at his mother for her abandonment.

And Sadie, for hers.

It had been the bitterest pill of all to swallow—the knowledge that he was subjecting his son to the same experience he'd had—growing up with no mother.

Sol spoke around the apple in his mouth and Quin put up a hand. 'Not with your mouth full, young man. Swallow and then speak.'

Sol did so, with such comic facial expressions that Quin had to bite his lip to stop himself from smiling.

As soon as he could speak, Sol said, 'Is Sadie gone?'

Quin felt a moment of trepidation. She might very well be gone. Maybe after she'd seen her son she had realised that actually, Quin's fortune notwithstanding, she didn't want to do this, and left again? Vanished into thin air.

There was such a mix of conflicting emotions at that idea that Quin said abruptly, 'Why don't you change out of your school clothes and put them in the laundry basket for Sara? If she has to pick them up from your floor again she said she's going to instruct Roberto to feed you nothing but zucchini for a whole week.'

Sol made a gagging sound—he hated zucchini—and ran to his room.

Quin put a hand through his hair. He went outside

and looked towards the trees that shielded the guest-house. He walked towards it, but as he did so memories rose up and threatened to swamp him. Memories of that fateful day when he'd returned to the little beach house where he and Sadie had lived together. He'd had days-old Sol in a harness, strapped to his chest. He'd taken him out for a walk to let Sadie get some rest after an early-morning feed.

When he'd returned to the house he'd been quiet, mindful of Sol sleeping against his chest, and also that Sadie might still be sleeping. But when he'd checked the bedroom, the bed had been empty.

Assuming she was in the bathroom, Quin had waited for a minute. But he'd heard nothing. Concern had grown and, imagining that something had happened, he'd called her name softly and opened the bathroom door—only to find that room empty too.

Maybe she'd gone to the beach?

Quin had gone out to the wraparound veranda and scanned the beach. No sign of Sadie. A sense of unease like nothing he'd ever experienced had crept along his skin. Somehow, he'd known in that moment that she was gone, and yet he hadn't admitted it to himself for some hours. Waiting. Feeding a fractious Sol with the expressed milk he'd found in the fridge.

It was only in the early afternoon that he'd found the note propped up against a mirror in the bedroom. The note that had struck him like a blow to the head, leaving him reeling.

Please believe me when I say I don't want to leave but I have to. Don't try to find me. Take care of Sol. I love you.

I love you. Quin let out a harsh sound. If that had been love then it had confirmed everything he'd been taught growing up. Love didn't exist. The only love he trusted now was the love he felt for his son.

Quin broke through the tree line and made his way to the guesthouse, telling himself that if Sadie had disappeared again she'd have done them all a huge favour. The fact that he was even feeling any kind of trepidation that she might be gone again irritated him intensely.

Sadie had finished unpacking her paltry belongings some time ago, after returning from lunch, during which Quin had mainly avoided her eye and said as little as possible.

She'd put a wash on—and it was embarrassing how much that had felt like such a treat. She'd explored the entirety of the guesthouse and been blown away again by its sheer opulence, albeit tastefully understated.

She'd showered and changed into soft, worn jeans and a clean T-shirt with short sleeves. She'd resisted the temptation to put her engagement-wedding ring back on her finger and instead had put it on a plain chain around her neck. She couldn't bear for it not to be touching her skin somewhere. It had become something of a talisman in the last four years, along with the picture of Quin holding Sol when he was a tiny baby.

She'd found a massive TV behind a sliding wooden door, along with a sound system. Books lined shelves—thrillers, literary fiction, commercial fiction, non-fiction. Sadie's fingers had itched to pick up one of the books—she hadn't had the mental headspace to do something as relaxing as reading in years. Four years. When she'd been with Quin she'd read voraciously.

Now she was in the bedroom. It was like an oasis of calm, with dark polished wood and soft textiles. Earthen colours. The massive bed looked so inviting that Sadie had no choice but to kick off her shoes and crawl onto it, groaning a little at the way it cushioned her body. Weariness crept over her...a bone-deep weariness. She felt the adrenalin of the last twenty-four hours finally draining from her system.

She was about to close her eyes when she heard a sound, and looked up to see Quin standing in the doorway. Instantly any sense of peace vanished and adrenalin flooded her system again.

She sat up and scooted off the bed. 'Sorry, I was just—'

'You don't have to apologise,' Quin said tightly. 'This is your space, and while you're here you're our guest. I should have knocked.'

The way Quin had looked at her since they'd met again—with something veering between disgust and severe distrust—made her wonder how much control it was taking for him to be so civil. But she didn't want to give him any excuse to kick her off his property. Out of their lives.

'Thank you,' she said. 'I do really appreciate that you're letting me stay.'

'Sol was asking if you were still here.'

Sadie's chest tightened at the mention of her son. 'I'm not going anywhere.'

Quin glanced at his watch. 'We'll have supper in about an hour.'

'Okay.' Sadie watched Quin leave and disappear back into the trees.

She sat down on the end of the bed, deflating. Absurd

to feel so hurt by Quin's coolness, especially after everything that had happened.

She was here now, and she was free to pursue a life with her son—that was all that mattered. Whatever bond she'd had with Quin was well and truly broken.

CHAPTER FOUR

QUIN DIDN'T LIKE the way it felt to hear Sadie's distinctively low-pitched voice mingling with Sol's more high-pitched excitable tone, both emanating from his bedroom, where Sol had demanded she come as soon as she'd appeared at the house a short while before.

It felt disturbing and arousing and a million things all at once.

He'd all but shut the door on Sadie ever being a part of their lives again. It was conflicting, inspiring too many things for him to unpick. But one stood out... The hum in his blood when he heard her now. The slow-burning lick of desire, coiling his insides tight.

It had been like that from the moment he'd seen her.

The first day he'd laid eyes on her would be seared onto his memory for ever, whether he liked it or not. He'd been living in Sao Sebastiao for a few months by then, and one day he'd noticed a young woman on the beach, in the water, surfing...or attempting to surf...inelegantly.

He'd been intrigued by her because she'd seemed to be by herself. No friends. Like him. He'd watched her attempt to catch waves, and fail, and then get up and try again. Her tenacity had impressed him.

As had her physicality. The slim, lithe limbs. Toned

muscles. He'd been able to tell she was pretty, even from a distance, but he'd had no idea how pretty until he'd seen her up close a couple of days later.

She'd disappeared from the beach after that first sighting, he'd thought he wouldn't see her again, until he'd walked into the local barber shop and she'd greeted him.

As soon as their eyes had met he'd felt it like a surge of electricity, all the way through his body. And he'd realised, *She's not pretty...she's beautiful.* Those wide aquamarine eyes, that straight nose, wide mouth. Dark hair...darker than it was now. Framing her face and making her look pale, in spite of the sun-kissed glow and freckles.

She'd cut his hair and it had felt like a more intimate act than sex. He hadn't been able to take his eyes off her. Her hands were small and deft, nails short. Unvarnished. And, against every instinct within him that had always told him not to trust women, there was something about Sadie, uniquely, that had lodged under his skin from that first meeting and started to dismantle all those defences without him even noticing.

He'd asked her out. But she'd declined. Not meeting his eye. He'd come back and asked her out again the next day. She'd blushed, but declined again, looking genuinely conflicted.

It had been the following day when he'd seen her trying to surf again and had witnessed the accident. She'd disappeared under the water for too long. He could remember the sense of panic as he'd raced to find her and pull her out of the water, giving her mouth-to-mouth resuscitation. The blood had flowed from a gash on her head.

When the emergency crew had arrived they'd just assumed he knew her, and without even questioning it he'd accompanied her to the hospital. When she'd woken, she'd frowned at Quin and said in a cracked voice, 'Do I know you?'

He'd almost been insulted—he knew he'd made an impression on her—but then it had transpired very quickly that she didn't remember anything at all from before the moment of the accident. Not her name or where she came from. She spoke with an English accent. *He* knew her name and where she worked because they'd met at the barber shop. When no one had come looking for her, Quin had offered to be the one to watch over her for the first few days after she left the hospital.

She'd had to be supervised, in case of further after-effects from her head injury. But, apart from the memory loss and the nasty gash on her head, there had been no further injuries or trauma.

Quin had taken her to the barber shop, where they'd told her where she lived, and they'd gone there—a small, modest studio apartment a few blocks from the beach. There had been no identifying things there, like pictures. Her mobile phone was gone—lost or stolen. The number had been inactive when he'd tried calling it. They'd found her passport, listing her as Sadie Ryan, twenty years old, with no next of kin. Born in Dublin, Ireland.

This had confused Sadie, and she'd said, 'That doesn't sound right. I don't have an Irish accent…and I don't think I've ever been there.'

The doctor had warned Quin not to let her get stressed, so he'd told her not to worry about it too much and that he'd look into trying to trace her and her family. Then they'd packed up her things so she could stay with him, as his beach bungalow had two bedrooms.

While she'd slept in the spare room he'd looked her up online and found no trace of her. Nothing. No social media presence. No records. No one seemed to be looking for her. Odd... But then a modest-sized city on the coast of Brazil, more akin to a sleepy beach town, was full of such nomads. He should have known—he was one of them.

He'd offered to put her details online with a picture, to advertise that she was looking for relatives, but she'd had the oddest reaction—one of almost fear. She'd said that she couldn't explain why, but she didn't want him to do that. So he hadn't.

He'd put Sadie's reluctance to be found and lack of online presence and any obvious family down to something that she could worry about when she got her memory back. He'd been able to empathise with her wanting to escape from her family, if that was the case.

As the days had passed she'd recovered from her injury in every other way except for her memory. She'd never moved back into her studio apartment. Finding out about her past had become less and less of a priority.

She'd never left Quin's side during those early days of recuperation. They'd become entwined. They'd fallen in love. And the outside world had fallen away...

Sadie laughed now—a low chuckle, bringing Quin out of the past. He shook his head, angry with himself for letting those memories intrude. He hadn't loved her. It had been infatuation borne out of lust.

He walked to the door of Sol's room and stopped. Sadie was sitting cross-legged on the floor and looking up at Sol, who was standing on his bed, pointing to a poster of his current football hero. She was wearing jeans and a T-shirt and her hair was pulled up into a loose knot on her head, tendrils falling around her face. Quin was once again struck by her natural beauty.

Sol was saying, 'Someday I'm going to be even better than him!'

Sadie smiled. 'I saw the goal posts in the garden—you must practise a lot.'

Sol saw Quin and jumped off the bed. He came straight over, launching himself at his father, arms around his waist. 'My papa is the best—he's practising with me every day after school.'

Sadie got to her feet in a fluid motion. Quin's pulse throbbed. She'd always been so naturally graceful. Except when it came to surfing. She'd never fully mastered the art, and had been too impatient, no matter what Quin said to her.

More memories.

He shoved them aside and said, more brusquely than he had intended, 'Dinner is ready.'

He saw the way Sadie's smile faltered at his tone. But Sol didn't notice the chill in the air and let Quin go, skipping downstairs. Quin refused to let those huge eyes affect him. He turned away, but couldn't deny how acutely conscious he was of Sadie as she followed him down to the kitchen-diner.

Roberto had prepared a light meal of pasta and sauce with salad and bread.

Sol grabbed some bread and Quin said, 'Ah-ah—not so fast. Let's try and pretend we're a little more civilised, hmm?'

Sol put the bread back with a sheepish look at Sadie and sat down. Quin avoided looking at her. A part of him didn't want to see how she was reacting to being with her son. Because he didn't know how to deal with it yet. The most important thing was to keep her close, where he could be sure of knowing exactly what she was up to...

Once they were all seated, Quin handed Sol the bread and said, '*Now* you can eat.'

Sol fell on the food, demonstrating his ravenous appetite.

Sadie ate too, with the healthy appetite that Quin remembered, cleaning her plate.

He couldn't help observing, 'You still eat fast.'

Sadie looked at him, eyes wide, a faint flush stealing into her cheeks.

Sol was indignant. 'I eat the fastest in this house.'

Quin welcomed the distraction from looking at Sadie and remembering too much. His tone was dry. 'It's not a race.'

When he was finished, Sol emitted a barely concealed burp.

Quin said, 'Okay, that's enough, young man. Take your plate into the kitchen and have a piece of fruit for dessert. You can play one game, and then I'm coming to get you ready for bed.'

Sol jumped up, and then stopped and looked at Sadie. 'Will you still be here tomorrow?'

Sadie's eyes were huge. Mirror images of her son's. It was almost laughable how alike they were. She glanced at Quin and he had to clamp down on his body's response.

She looked at Sol. 'I think so. I'm hoping to stay for as long as you'll have me.'

'Cool! See you tomorrow! Do you know how to play football? I'll show you. Night!'

He disappeared up to his room in a blur of motion. Sadie looked at Quin. She seemed a little dazed.

Eventually she said, 'He's an amazing kid. You're a good father, Quin.'

'I had no choice.'

Her mouth tightened. 'Parents have a choice, no matter what the circumstances. You could have easily outsourced his care, but clearly you haven't. And Madalena seems to be almost like a grandmother to him.'

Quin made a snorting noise. 'There's no harm in that. He's never met his real grandmother.' He looked at Sadie. 'Either of them.'

She went pale. 'You know that I had no idea if I had any family or not...'

Quin arched a brow. *'Had?'*

He could see Sadie go even paler, visibly swallowing. 'Actually...that's what I need to talk to you about.... to explain why—'

'Papa! The game isn't working! Can you make it work?'

Unnoticed, Sol had reappeared by the dining table and was holding up a console.

Quin cursed silently and stood up. He wasn't sure he'd ever be ready to hear why Sadie had left so precipitously, but he knew he had to. Maybe not right now, though.

He said to Sol, 'Go back upstairs. I'll come up in a minute.'

When Sol had left, he looked at Sadie. 'We can't talk about this now. I'll be busy getting Sol to bed in a bit, so help yourself to anything else you'd like from the kitchen.

Lights will come on in the garden to guide you back to the guesthouse. I'll see you tomorrow.'

Sadie stood up and picked up her plate and Quin's, but he said, 'Leave them. Roberto will clean up in the morning. Sara would normally be here, but she's out of action.'

She put the plates back down. 'Your housekeeper? Did something happen?'

'She was involved in an accident today and she'll be out of work for a week. It shouldn't inconvenience you too much.'

Sadie looked genuinely concerned. 'That's awful… is she okay?'

Quin didn't like this reminder of Sadie's compassionate nature. Because it had obviously been false. No genuinely compassionate person could walk away from their baby. Or the man they'd professed to love.

He said, 'Her car was totalled but she's okay—just shaken. I gave her a week off to recover…'

Sadie gestured to the plates. 'I'll do this. I don't mind—honestly. And I can do whatever else she was meant to be doing. It'll give me a way to say thank you… for letting me be here.'

Quin felt a strong sense of rejection at the thought of Sadie doing his domestic chores—but then this wasn't a regular situation. And there was also a little devil inside him that relished the thought of calling her bluff, to see if she really meant it. He had to admit, the notion of her doing menial work as some sort of recompense wasn't altogether undesirable. The rage inside him that still burned bright for what she'd done demanded to be appeased.

But he said, 'Are you sure? There's no need. Between me, Roberto and Lena we can manage.'

Sadie shook her head. 'I'm sure they're busy enough. I insist—it's the least I can do.'

Quin shrugged. 'Suit yourself. Roberto will fill you in on Sara's duties when he comes in tomorrow. Goodnight, Sadie.'

'Are you sure this is okay?'

Lena was looking at Sadie with concern in her eyes. But Sadie couldn't have been more sure that she wanted to keep herself busy. What else was she going to do in her lush isolation among the trees?

She nodded. 'Honestly, it's fine. I'd like to help out.'

Lena obviously wasn't convinced. 'But you're—'

She stopped, clearly not wanting to state the obvious. Yet. The fact that Sadie was Sol's mother, who had reappeared after four years of abandonment. That, as his mother, she shouldn't be working like an employee.

Sadie forced a smile. 'I'm happy to be here. And happy to be of use.'

Lena finally gave in and pushed a Tupperware box towards Sadie. 'You can pack up Sol's lunch, then, if that's okay? And I'll make sure he's getting dressed.' She rolled her eyes, 'He's probably playing one of his games…'

Sadie's heart squeezed as the woman left the kitchen. That should be *her* job—chasing Sol to get ready for school. But she didn't have that privilege yet. Would she ever?

The way Quin had looked at her last night did not bode well. He'd tolerated her presence and that had been about it. She supposed she should be glad that he was even allowing her to come and eat with them. Not confining her to the guesthouse.

She'd come up to the house early this morning, hoping that she might get to continue her aborted conversation with Quin. Give him the explanation of why she'd left. But she'd found Roberto clearing up after breakfast. He'd told her that Quin was in the home office, making calls, and that Sol was getting ready for school. He'd looked at her quizzically when she'd told him she was going to fill in for Sara, but he'd said nothing—just told her that he'd go over her duties once Sol had left for school. Then he'd insisted on her having breakfast, and had made her a delicious plate of scrambled eggs, ham and chives.

Sadie felt pathetically grateful that Roberto and Lena didn't seem to be judging her for her absence.

She'd just closed the lid on the Tupperware lunchbox when Sol appeared in front of her, as if conjured out of her imagination. He looked smart in his shorts and school T-shirt. Hair smoothed.

He smiled. 'You're still here.'

Her heart squeezed again. 'Yes.'

He touched a tooth in his mouth. 'I have a loose tooth.'

Sadie came around the table and bent down. She could see it wobble. 'If it comes out you'll have to leave it under your pillow for the tooth fairy.'

Sol frowned. 'What's a tooth fairy? We leave it out for the bird, and the bird leaves a gift. Your tooth has to be really clean, so I cleaned extra-hard today, but it still didn't come out.'

Sadie bit back a smile and stood up. 'Ah…where I came from the tooth fairy takes the tooth from under your pillow and leaves a surprise, but I like the sound of a special bird.'

'Where *did* you come from?'

That question hadn't come from Sol. It had come from someone much more adult.

Sadie looked up to see Quin. She couldn't find her breath for a moment...he was so stupendously gorgeous. Clean-shaven. Hair still damp from the shower. Dressed in a shirt open at the neck, sleeves rolled up. Faded jeans.

It had only been around thirty-six hours since they'd met again, and yet it felt all at once like years and no time at all. Apart from that reference to a grandmother last night, Quin hadn't yet mentioned her memory loss, or asked about it, but was he ready to hear what she had to say now? Was *she* ready?

'Don't you know where Sadie comes from, Papa?'

But Quin didn't look at Sol. Sadie swallowed. Did he really want to do this here? Now? In front of their son?

She was about to answer, but then Quin broke the intense eye contact and said, 'We'd better get moving, Sol. I'm going to drop you to school today.'

'Yay! I'll get my bag.'

'See you out front in five minutes.'

Sol disappeared again, and now it was just Quin and Sadie. He arched a brow. Clearly waiting for an answer.

Sadie said in a husky voice, 'I was born and brought up in England, just outside London.'

Something flashed across his face. 'So your memory came back...or was it ever really gone?'

Sadie gulped. She'd never considered that he might doubt she'd really lost her memory. 'Yes, it came back.'

'So, you're not Irish, then?'

'Well...my father was Irish. But I never lived there.'

'But you had an Irish passport?'

Yes, she had. But she hadn't grown up with an Irish

passport. She'd actually grown up with *no* passport. She'd only got her first passport to come to Brazil.

She opened her mouth again but Sol reappeared, trailing a small bag. 'Okay, Papa, I'm ready.'

Quin's jaw clenched. But then he said, 'Okay, let's go.' And then to Sadie he said, 'Lena and Roberto will show you the ropes. I'll be out at a function later, and Sol is going to a sleepover, so we'll see you tomorrow.'

Sol was already running out through the door. 'Bye, Sadie!'

Sadie said a very faint 'Bye…' as she watched them leave, feeling all at once frustrated and relieved that her attempt to explain everything to Quin had been interrupted again.

Later that night Quin was not in a good mood as he took a swig of alcohol from the thick crystal tumbler in his hand. He was staring out through the massive glass wall of his living area, down to where he could just make out the guesthouse, illuminated through the trees.

He'd just endured a function in central Sao Paulo where all the women seemed to have made it a national sport to get his attention. His mouth tightened cynically. Amazing what becoming a billionaire could do for your eligibility.

Not that he'd ever *not* been eligible, he had to concede, with no sense of hubris.

He'd been distracted all evening—and not just by the women seeking his attention. He'd been distracted because he hadn't been able to get one woman out of his head. The woman who had haunted him for four years. The woman who was no longer a ghost but very much alive and breathing—and existing mere metres from where he stood now.

That night in New York he'd finally been ready to cut her ghost and her memory loose. To get on with his life, take a lover… Only for her to appear in the flesh, thwarting him and setting him back. Four years.

He'd just had a conversation with Lena, who'd told him, 'She knows her way around cleaning a house and doing laundry—that much is obvious. But, Quin—'

Before she'd been able to say anything more—like demanding to know what the hell was going on with this woman who had just appeared and who looked ridiculously like Sol—he'd terminated the conversation and she'd left to go back to her own house.

He didn't like it that his conscience was prickling with the knowledge that he was keeping something huge from the two people who had been more of a family to him than his own family, and the fact that the mother of his child had been doing menial chores around his house.

It all mixed together with the residual anger, hurt, confusion, distrust…and *lust*…to make a volatile mix.

He swallowed the rest of the drink and took off his bow tie. He opened his top button, feeling constricted. Restless. He could keep drinking and brooding, or he could go and confront the woman who was lodged in his side like a burr.

He pulled off his jacket, dropped it on a chair, then pulled back the glass door and went outside. The air was warm. Soft. When he felt hard. Prickly.

He walked down through the garden, and as he came closer to the trees and the guesthouse he could hear the soft strains of familiar music. But not that familiar… He hadn't heard it in four years.

He came to a stop in the trees as the sensual voice of a well-known Brazilian jazz singer washed over him. For a crazy second he wondered if he was losing his mind. Had he hallucinated Sadie back into his life and now he was hearing things? She'd loved this artist and had used to play her all the time. She'd given birth to Sol with this music in the background.

He kept moving forward until he could see the house. Low lights were on, but he couldn't see any sign of Sadie. He walked around and saw the front door was open. The music was louder now.

He walked inside and could smell her scent. Not a ghost, then. He went over to the sound system in the den area and pressed the *off* button. Silence enclosed him.

Then from behind him a voice said, 'You used to say that I played her too much.'

Quin turned around and the blood rushed straight to his head. Sadie was standing before him in a short, belted robe. Long bare legs. Pale. Hair damp and falling in golden-red skeins around her shoulders.

He dimly realised she must have been swimming, just as she gestured with her hand behind her and said, 'I hope you don't mind… I had a swim.'

He shook his head, but everything had turned fuzzy. He couldn't take his eyes off her. Off the vee of skin exposed by the robe…the hint of plump cleavage.

Blood thundered through his veins. It had been so long. She'd tortured him for four years with X-rated dreams that had left him aching and frustrated. He'd been tortured by endless questions. *Why? Why? Why?*

Why? Why? Why? Yet now she was here in front of him, and he could actually ask her *why*, Quin perversely didn't want to know. It was as if he'd intuited that once he knew *why* he would no longer have anything to hold on to.

The hatred. The justifiable anger. The pain. *The loss.*

He moved towards her as if pulled by a magnetic force. He couldn't *not*. She looked at him, eyes wide. That mesmerising shade of blue and green. Depths he'd drowned in. But no more. There would be no drowning this time.

She spoke. 'Quin…we should talk. Maybe now is good because Sol is away tonight. We have time—'

Quin put his hands on her arms and the words stopped. Good. He didn't want words. Except to say, 'I don't want to talk right now. All I want is *this*.'

He pulled her into his body, where she fitted like a missing jigsaw piece, slotting into place against him. He lowered his head and took a breath as he closed his eyes and slanted his mouth over hers, and everything inside him turned to heat and fire and longing and an almost unbearable demand for satisfaction. It had been so long… and he'd never stopped wanting her.

Any recrimination he might have felt for giving in to this weakness was burnt to ashes in the conflagration of their kiss.

CHAPTER FIVE

SADIE WAS RIGID against Quin for a long moment. It was the shock of being in his arms again after so long. The shock of his mouth on hers…all at once familiar and utterly new. But the shock was fast dissolving under his touch, being replaced with a desire and a hunger so deep and ravenous that within seconds she was pressing closer, twining her arms around his neck and stretching up as much as she could, so she could meet his kiss with a desperation that clawed up from the centre of her body and spread out to every limb, making her shake with it.

They ceased to be bodies. They were heat and need and intense burning desire. Quin's hands were on her robe, undoing the belt, pushing it off her shoulders so it fell to the floor. His fingers were under her swimsuit straps, pushing them off and down, then the wet material was being peeled from her body to fall to the floor.

He broke the kiss and pulled back, stood up straight.

Sadie was unselfconscious in her nakedness—she needed Quin too much. His dark gaze feasted on her flesh, taking in every dip and hollow. She was filled with urgency and reached for him, undoing the buttons on his shirt, breath fast, panicky with need, in case this moment somehow dissolved and she lost him again.

You didn't lose him...you walked away, reminded a little voice.

Sadie ignored it. Clearly Quin was not ready to hear what she had to say, and maybe she still wasn't ready to tell him either. There was so much unspoken between them and maybe this was the only way to defuse it. Then maybe they could talk like rational adults.

Quin was naked now. Sadie wasn't aware of having removed his trousers and underwear. Maybe he had. But she didn't care. She felt as if she could finally breathe again.

She reached out and touched his chest, putting her hands to his warm skin. Her fingers trapped his nipples, the light dusting of hair over his pectorals. Her gaze took in the lean muscles of his stomach and down, to narrow hips and the place where he was magnificent and proud. *Hard* for her.

She wrapped a hand around him and heard his indrawn breath. She looked up and felt dizzy. His face was stark with the same need that was coursing through her own blood.

He took her hand off him and said, 'No time. I need you now.'

He took Sadie's hand and she let herself be led into the bedroom. Quin let her go for a moment, disappearing into the bathroom. Sadie sat down on the bed, her legs weak. She was trembling all over. She couldn't believe this was happening. Was it a dream?

Quin reappeared, his tall, muscular body gleaming like burnished bronze in the low lights. He'd always been supremely at ease naked. That was helped by the fact that he was more beautiful than any man could be, but also because he had an innate confidence that Sadie had always envied.

Now she knew it came from being brought up as a member of one America's most venerated families. Something he'd kept from her. Her guts twisted. They had so much to discuss… But, weakly, she pushed it all aside and watched as Quin rolled a protective sheath onto his erection.

She hadn't known there was protection in the bathroom. Did he use this house when he brought lovers over? That had to be it. To keep his home and personal life separate. A little knife lodged in her heart as she thought of him taking lovers here, but of course she had no right to be hurt. Not after what she'd done.

Then Quin stood before her and every thought went out of her head.

He said, 'Move back on the bed.'

Sadie somehow managed to get her limbs to move. She lay back and watched as Quin came over her, muscles rippling. She remembered how it had always been between them. So intense. She quivered inwardly. Was she ready for this again? She'd never be ready… But she knew she needed it like she needed oxygen. To keep breathing. To stay alive.

Quin looked at her, and she felt the flush of blood rising to her skin under his gaze.

He said roughly, 'You haven't changed.'

Sadie would have refuted that if she'd been able to speak. She felt like a different person. She'd broken inside when she'd had to walk away from Quin and Sol, and she didn't know if those jagged pieces would ever heal. But he wouldn't want to hear that.

'You haven't changed either,' she said, feeling shy for a second.

His gaze met hers and she almost gasped at the swirling vortex of emotion she glimpsed before he lowered his lids and masked his eyes from her. Maybe he had changed too. Although, as much as he'd told her he loved her *before*, she couldn't imagine that he'd loved her more than she had him. And that love had certainly died with her disappearance.

He rested on his hands over her, his body long and sleek. Jaw stubbled. Mouth tempting. To stop any more thoughts intruding, and robbing her of this moment, Sadie reached up for him. 'Please, Quin. I need you.'

He hesitated for a moment, and Sadie had a few seconds of blood-curdling fear that he'd planned on bringing her to the brink like this only to humiliate her at the last moment. The old Quin she'd known wouldn't have ever done anything so cruel, but this man was not the same. Physically, maybe, but in every other way not the same.

But he put an arm under her back, arching her up to him. Sadie widened her legs around him, tacitly telling him what she wanted. She bit her lip. And then before she could take another breath Quin was sliding into her.

She gasped at the sensation. She'd forgotten what it was like…and yet she'd forgotten nothing. He was stretching her wide, and it had been four years, so it bordered on being painful.

Quin stopped. 'Sadie?'

But she could already feel the way her body was accommodating him, relearning his shape, accepting him.

Breathless, she said, 'It's fine… I'm fine. Don't stop… *please*.'

Slowly he started to move…in and out. An age-old dance. He was the only man she'd ever slept with, and she had to bury her head in Quin's shoulder for a moment, in case he saw the emotion bubbling upwards at the realisation that she wanted him to be the only man she ever slept with. Forever.

But that was a dream she had no right to now.

All she had was this present moment.

Mercifully, the sensations in her body were eclipsing the emotion as their movements became faster, more hungry. Sweat slicked their skin. Desperation clawed at Sadie's insides as the shimmering peak of ecstasy appeared on the horizon, her body quickening and tightening in anticipation.

She vaguely heard Quin mutter something under his breath—some kind of curse… Maybe because he wanted to eke out this moment but couldn't. Sadie could well imagine that Quin would relish torturing her as long as possible.

But the frenzy was upon them, and Sadie knew from previous experience that all she could do was surrender to it and let it sweep her away.

And that was exactly what happened. Quin thrust so deep that Sadie arched her back and wrapped her legs and arms around him, breaking apart all over and splintering into a million shards of pleasure.

She clung on for dear life as she felt Quin's big body jerk against hers as he found his own release, before he slumped over her, his face buried in her neck.

In that moment, Sadie felt the first measure of peace she'd had in four years.

* * *

When Sadie woke, she felt as if she was climbing up through several layers of sleep. She cracked open her eyes and squinted a little at the bright sunlight. She took in her surroundings—the spacious room, lots of glass, teak.

The guesthouse. Quin.

Instantly she was wide awake and registering that she was alone.

She sat up, holding the sheet to her chest. The bed was very rumpled but there was no dent in the pillow beside her, so Quin obviously hadn't gone to sleep here.

It all came rushing back. She'd taken a swim and had come back into the house to see Quin standing in the room. He'd switched off the music.

Music that had made her feel emotional as she heard it again, transporting her back to those halcyon days in Sao Sebastiao in their little beach hut, so wrapped up in each other that the outside world had gone unnoticed.

The music that Sol had been born to at exactly the same moment her head had been filled with restored memories and images and a horrific realisation. Two profound things happening at once.

Obviously she'd had to prioritise devoting all her energy into giving birth, ensuring her baby's safe passage into a world that was suddenly not a benign place any more. But from that moment on she'd been on borrowed time.

Sadie shook her head to free it of the past. She was here now. With her son. Well, not exactly *with* him, but in his world. And last night had just been a conflagration of the tension between her and Quin. Not helpful to their situation. Quite possibly he would resent her for this. Maybe he would see it as a weakness—giving in to the chemistry that was still between them.

If emotion had been involved on Quin's side Sadie was sure it wasn't any positive emotion. For her, though, it had been incredibly overwhelming, reminding her of the pull she'd felt as soon as she'd met him face to face for the first time.

Although, as she well knew, she'd felt that pull after spotting him on the porch of his house on the beach a couple of days before that. He'd been a solitary figure. Like her. Tall, compelling. Beautiful. But she'd done her best not to look him, to pretend that he hadn't caught her eye. Because she hadn't been able to afford to make connections with anyone. It was too dangerous.

But then he'd walked into the little barber shop where she'd worked, and she'd had nowhere to hide nor time to pretend she hadn't seen him. Within minutes she'd had his head in her hands. Running her fingers through his hair. Trying her best to avoid those dark, mesmerising eyes in the mirror. That sculpted mouth that had made her press her thighs together to stem the heat rising deep in her core.

He'd asked her out and her heart had leapt. For the first time she'd resented her life. She'd wished she could say *yes*, even though the thought had terrified her because he was so intimidatingly gorgeous and sexy. In any case, she hadn't had a choice. She'd had to say no.

The next day he'd reappeared and asked her out again. She'd said no again, even more regretful.

And then the next thing she remembered was waking

in hospital after the surfing accident…with nothing but a persistent fog in her head.

After that they'd never been apart again—until the moment she'd walked away. Out of his and her son's lives.

Sadie got out of the bed and pulled on a robe. Between her legs she felt tender. She blushed. Ridiculous. She took a shower and noticed the places on her body and skin where Quin's stubble had made it red, or where he'd squeezed her flesh.

She turned the shower to cold for a second, hoping to shock some sense back into her brain. Last night had meant nothing. Only that the desire between them was as strong as ever. Except…

Sadie shivered a little as she turned off the water. Maybe last night was all Quin had needed to exorcise her from his system.

When Quin returned from work later that day he wasn't prepared for the sight before him on the lawn. Sadie, in jeans and a T-shirt, battered sneakers, her hair pulled up, was playing football with Sol. She might have passed for a teenager if it hadn't been for her womanly curves.

He'd walked out of the guesthouse as dawn had broken that morning, telling himself that he wouldn't touch Sadie again. It had been a moment of madness. A build-up of four years of frustration and pain and anger.

He'd hoped that maybe now he'd feel some kind of peace.

But far from feeling any measure of peace, he'd been tormented by her all day. He'd kept having flashbacks to seeing her naked for the first time in four years. The way it had felt to slide into her body…the moment when she'd looked at him with wide eyes, reminding him of how she'd looked at him when they'd first made love because she'd been a virgin.

A question had buzzed in his head all day. Had she looked at him like that, had her body been so tight, because she hadn't slept with anyone in four years? Since him?

He hated it that he even cared.

Sadie expertly deflected the ball from Sol. Quin realised she was good. Sol was in heaven with such a worthy adversary, trying to get the ball back, and Quin could see the exact moment when she feigned missing it so that Sol could get it and shoot for the goal. He jumped up and down with glee and Sadie caught him around the waist and lifted him up. The two heads were close together, strawberry-blonde.

And suddenly it was too much—last night and now this.

Quin called out from the open door, 'Sol, time to clean up for dinner.'

Sadie turned around with Sol still in her arms and the two sets of aquamarine eyes hit him like a sledgehammer to the gut, compounding the sense of exposure he felt at having indulged in his lust for Sadie last night. And the way she'd dominated his thoughts all day.

He still didn't even know what her agenda was. Or why she'd walked out four years ago.

You didn't give her a chance to talk last night, reminded a little voice.

It made him call out again with uncharacteristic sharpness, 'Sol, *now*. I won't ask again.'

Sol slid down from Sadie's arms and came inside, looking at Quin warily, making him feel about two inches tall. He rarely, if ever, spoke harshly to his son.

He looked at Sadie and felt the impulse to blame her—but that wasn't fair either, in spite of everything.

She said, 'Sorry, that was probably my fault. I didn't realise how much time had passed.'

She had dirt on the knees of her jeans, and Quin could see a streak across one cheek. He couldn't imagine any of the kind of women he met now allowing themselves to get so dishevelled. But Sadie had never been concerned with her appearance—except for that weird habit she'd had, insisting on dyeing her hair once a month.

He'd asked her once, 'Why do you bother?'

If anything, it had only made her look more pale, and there was no reason to do it that he'd been able to understand.

She'd said, 'It's the weirdest thing, and I can't explain it, but I feel safer if I do it…'

Because of her memory loss they'd both put things like this down to quirks that might one day be explained.

He pushed the past back and said, 'It's fine.' And then, 'You should probably wash too…before dinner.'

Sadie put a hand to her face and blushed. She still blushed.

She said, 'Of course. But I just need to finish a couple of jobs first.'

She'd walked by Quin into the house before he could stop her, trailing her tantalising scent behind her—earth and roses and citrus. Clean, innocent…

Irritation and frustration prickled over and under Quin's skin at so many different things that before he could expose himself any more he set off to check on Sol—who was his priority above anything else. Or any-*one* else. Especially her.

Sadie was left in no doubt that Quin deeply regretted what had happened the previous night. The look he'd given her when he'd found her playing football with Sol had almost cut her in half.

Maybe she shouldn't have indulged in playing with her son, but when he'd come home from school with Lena he'd asked if she could play football with him. She'd explained regretfully that she still had some housework to do, but Lena had pooh-poohed that and told Sol to get changed into his kit.

Sadie couldn't feel sorry, though, because the last couple of hours had healed so much of the hurt and pain she'd endured. Her little boy was a joy. Sunny and mischievous and kind and funny. More than she'd even imagined he could be. Talking non-stop, endlessly curious...

Now Sadie quickly finished up what she'd been doing—sorting clothes in the laundry—and went back out to the main living-dining area, steeling herself in case she bumped into Quin and his disapproving expression again.

But Roberto was there, smiling. 'Dinner will be ready in a short while.'

Sadie's heartstrings were plucked. She'd love to spend more time with Sol, but she knew when she wasn't welcome. Sol had been away last night, and no doubt Quin would want to have him to himself.

She forced a smile. 'Thank you so much, but I'll eat in the guesthouse this evening.'

Roberto remonstrated with her, but Sadie insisted. However, he wouldn't let her go without giving her a portion of his stew in a Tupperware container. Sadie took it, touched again by his and Lena's kindness.

Before Sol had come back down earlier, still in his football kit, Sadie had said, 'I hope I'm not intruding too much on your routine with Sol?'

The older woman had shaken her head. 'Not at all. It's good you are here.'

Sadie had bitten her lip, and then blurted out, 'Thank you…you have no idea how much that means to me.'

Lena had taken Sadie's hand in hers and said, 'Some women are capable of walking away from a child, but I don't think you are. I'm sure you had a good reason to do what you did.'

Surprise at hearing her confirm that she did know that she was Sol's mother and at her words had taken Sadie's breath, and by the time she'd felt remotely able to respond Sol had returned and Lena had disappeared with a small wink.

Sadie said, 'Thank you,' again to Roberto, and left the house, walking back down through the garden to the guesthouse. She'd only been here for a couple of days, but the place already felt more like home than anywhere else she'd been.

Except for Sao Sebastiao.

Her and Quin's beach paradise.

She'd never wanted to leave. She hadn't even wanted to go into Sao Paulo to give birth. But Quin had insisted, strangely paranoid about the risks of childbirth.

It was only in the last four years that Sadie had realised that maybe on some level, in spite of her memory loss, she'd known that it would be inherently dangerous to go out of their cocooned existence at the beach and into a big city. Maybe going into the city had been the thing that had precipitated her memory return, and then Sol's birth had brought it back completely?

She was inside the guesthouse now, and she set up a place for herself at the dining table and tried not to look towards the trees, where the lights of the big house were just visible. She'd spent too many days and evenings walking around towns and cities in the last four years, glimpsing scenes of families together, and she wasn't going to allow herself to wallow in that self-pity again. She was free, and she was here—near to her son.

She pushed down the rising panic at the thought that she might always exist like this, on the margins of their lives. It was enough. It would have to be.

But a couple of hours later Sadie couldn't settle. She'd tried watching TV, but couldn't understand Portuguese. She'd tried reading, but had thrown the book down when she'd realised she'd read the same paragraph ten times without understanding a word.

It was rising within her. The need to tell Quin what had happened. He had to know. *Now.* The lights were still on in the house, visible through the trees. Yet she felt reluctant to go up there—especially as Quin hadn't appeared to invite her to join them.

Or to make love to you again, whispered a little voice.

Sadie cursed herself. That had been an incendiary moment, borne out of their tangled past and chemistry. An anomaly.

But in spite of her reluctance and misgivings, she pulled a light cardigan over her T-shirt and left the guesthouse.

All was quiet when she reached the house. No sign of anyone. She guessed Roberto and Lena would have gone home. Sol must be in bed. Maybe Quin was in bed too?

But then she heard a noise coming from the area where his office was situated and followed the sound. The door was partially open and light spilled out. Her heart thumped. She curbed the urge to turn and run. It was time to do this.

She knocked lightly on the door.

Quin's voice came. 'Sol? I told you that it's too late for—'

The words stopped when he opened the door and saw Sadie.

'Not Sol. It's me.'

He just looked at her for a long moment. 'Why didn't you come to dinner?'

She pushed aside the lingering feeling of loneliness. It was ridiculous, *she'd* made that decision to eat alone. In four years she'd not succumbed to self—pity and she wasn't about to start.

'I thought you'd appreciate time with Sol because he was away last night.'

And they'd made love. Heat threatened to rise at the memory. But then Sadie went cold inside as she wondered if she was so desperate for him to touch her again that *this* was the reason she'd come up here looking for him, not because she wanted to unburden herself about why she'd left.

He said, 'You would have been welcome.' Then he frowned. 'Is everything okay?'

Sadie swallowed. Whatever her reasons for coming

here, there was only one thing she really needed to do right now. 'I think we need to talk about what happened.'

Quin's expression turned to stone. 'That was a mistake. It won't happen again.'

Now Sadie frowned, confused. And then she realised what he was referring to. Last night. The recent past— not *the* past. A pain lanced her heart. Well, if she'd been in any doubt about how he felt about it, she wasn't now.

Feeling defensive, she said, 'You came to me.'

'I'm aware of that. Put it down to a certain level of frustration.'

Charming. He'd only slept with her because she'd been convenient, in spite of all of their baggage.

Forgetting momentarily why she'd come, Sadie said, 'So does that mean you haven't had any lovers?'

He looked at her. 'I told you I wasn't with anyone.'

A little rogue devil inside Sadie somersaulted. Maybe if he hadn't been with anyone then he didn't despise her as much as he wanted her to believe. 'I wasn't sure if that meant lovers or a relationship.'

'Like I said, I don't have much time to focus on a personal life.'

Sadie realised they'd got way off track. She shook her head. 'That's not what I came to talk to you about. You misunderstood me.'

'What *did* you come to talk about?'

She steeled herself. 'I think now is as good a time as any to tell you why I left.'

For a long moment Quin said nothing. She half expected him to say it was too late.

But then he stood back to admit her into the office and said, 'I guess it is.'

Nerves assailed Sadie as she walked into the large room, but she couldn't back out now. She hadn't taken in all that much detail in when she'd seen the room before, but now she noticed the hardwood floors softened by colourful rugs. Floor-to-ceiling shelves groaned with books. There was a huge desk and a plethora of computers and devices. Touchingly, in one corner there was a kiddie-sized table and chair—evidence of Quin having Sol close by while he was working. Making him feel included.

Quin walked around to the other side of his desk and folded his arms and looked at her. 'Go on, Sadie, I'm all ears.'

He wasn't making this easy. Needing some courage in the face of his lack of emotion, not to mention his rejection of what had happened the previous night, she asked, 'Do you have anything to drink in here?'

Quin unlocked his arms. 'That's not a bad idea.'

As she watched, he went over to a cabinet in the corner of the room, and she saw him open a bottle and pour dark golden liquid into two small glasses. He came back and handed her one.

He lifted his glass and said, 'Cheers,' then downed his drink in one.

Sadie echoed his *'cheers'* faintly, and did the same as him, wincing as the bitter liquid burned its way down her throat and into her belly. But it had an effect, sending out a warming glow that automatically made her feel less…edgy.

'You never did like hard spirits much,' he observed.

He remembered.

How much else did he remember? Would he ever just remember the good times?

Quin took the glass out of her hand and said, 'Another?'

Sadie shook her head. 'No, that's enough.'

He put the glasses back and turned around again, folding his arms. 'Well?'

It was unbelievably daunting, having to launch into explaining everything while Quin exuded such remoteness.

'Can you…not look at me like that, please?'

'Like what?'

Like we weren't making love just twenty-four hours ago.

Sadie shook her head. 'Nothing. It's just…a lot to tell you. And I'm nervous. Can we sit down, or something?'

'Of course.'

Quin felt so tense he thought he might crack. He had to consciously breathe and relax his muscles, but it was hard when all he could do was look at Sadie and want her. In spite of what he'd just told her.

'It won't happen again.'

His brain might have formulated those words but his body did not agree. His blood was hot and heavy in his veins. And his groin.

She looked incredibly fragile right now. Pale. She'd changed into soft, worn sweat pants and another nondescript T-shirt, with a cardigan pulled across her chest. Her hair was still messy from earlier. But she was no less alluring than she'd been last night, when they'd come together like two starving people in the desert finding water.

When she hadn't come for dinner he'd told himself it was a good thing. Since she'd reappeared in their lives he hadn't felt fully in control. He'd been behaving instinctively. Reacting. The previous night was proof of that.

So he'd ignored the urge to go and get her, and had told Sol she needed to have some time for herself. He had done his best not to notice his son's disappointment. But he'd been conscious of the guesthouse lights through the trees.

He'd had to shut himself away in his office after he'd put Sol to bed, because the urge to go to her again had been so strong.

And even now, when she was about to tell him why she had walked out of their lives, he still couldn't focus fully. Damn her.

He forced his blood to cool and said, with as much civility as he could, 'Please, sit down.'

He pulled out a chair and Sadie sat, stiff. She was obviously as tense as him. He forced himself to sit too, on a chair near her, and rejected an urge he had to tug her onto his lap and feel her close to him, to reassure her that she could tell him anything.

This was why he couldn't touch her again. It clouded his brain. And he needed to be very clear now, when she was about to tell him why she'd walked out on her newborn baby and him. As far as Quin was concerned there was no reason on earth that could justify why she'd done that.

'Can you stop glaring at me? This is hard enough.'

Quin cursed silently and forced himself to relax. She

was clasping and unclasping her hands. She was nervous. She was avoiding his eye now.

'Look, what I'm going to tell you is going to be a lot to take in and it's going to sound…ridiculous.'

She looked at him, and Quin's insides clenched at the sight of those amazing eyes.

'But it's all true. I promise you.'

The only true thing Quin knew in that moment was that, no matter what lurid tale fell out of this woman's mouth now, he would never trust her again.

He sat back and forced his tense limbs to relax. 'Go on, please.'

CHAPTER SIX

Now Sadie couldn't sit still. She stood up and started to pace. Where did she even start?

'Sadie?'

She looked at Quin, who was leaning forward. This was it. No more hiding or procrastinating. She stopped pacing and took a breath.

'In the year before we met…before I came to Brazil… I was working in a big house in London for a very rich man. I was a housemaid—one of dozens. The house was huge…luxurious…like nothing I'd ever seen. The owner wasn't English, his accent hard to place. We hardly ever saw him. We weren't allowed to look at him, in any case.'

She started to pace again.

'One evening, I thought I'd forgotten to check that the lunch things had been taken out of his office—he was a stickler for that kind of thing. I was due to go home, and I didn't want the girl taking over from me to get in trouble, so I went back to the office before I left, to check.

'When I got to the door, it was partially open, and I pushed it open all the way. I saw that the owner was inside, with his back to me. It took me a minute to understand what I was looking at. There was a man on the floor in front of him, on his knees, with his hands tied behind his

back. He was begging, pleading… I could see his face…
he was young… I didn't recognise him. I saw my boss…
the owner…take something out of the back of his trousers
and hold it to the man's forehead. And then there was a
sound…like a loud but muffled crack. I didn't recognise
it at first—it was such an odd thing to hear. But then I realised that he'd shot him. Just like that. Without even hesi-
tating. I'll never forget the mark on the man's forehead,
or the way he fell backwards. And then the blood…bright
red…so much blood…all around his head, on the floor…'

Sadie stopped pacing and looked at Quin, not really
registering his expression.

'I must have made a sound, or something, because my
boss turned around. He was still holding the gun, and it
was pointing at me now. I could see him taking in that
it was me, just a member of staff. Maybe he knew who
I was…maybe he didn't. But somehow I felt in that moment that he knew exactly who I was, and that I had no
family, no ties. He could shoot me and no one would ever
know. So I ran. All the way out of the house, out through
the gate, onto the road. I kept running until I ran straight
into a man who bundled me into a van. I thought it was
someone attached to him. I was terrified. But it was the
police…or not the police…a specialist unit. They'd been
watching the house…they saw me run.'

Sadie stopped. She felt a little light-headed. She'd only
ever told this once to the police, and then again for her
video witness statement. She'd never told another soul.

Quin was looking at her. His face was hard. 'Is there
more?'

Sadie swallowed. He didn't believe her. But she'd
started now.

She sat down again on the edge of the chair, hands clasped in her lap. 'The police…detectives…whoever they were, took me to a police station—except it wasn't like any I'd seen before. It turned out the man I worked for was a well-known name in the organised crime world. Up to that point he'd never been caught doing anything himself—he was too powerful. The fact that I'd witnessed him murdering someone himself, on his own property, turned out to be their big break. But he fled the country before they could catch him.'

Sadie stood and paced again.

'I knew there was something off about the house—and the people in it but I didn't take much notice because I was only there to work part-time, to help pay for my hairdressing course. The man's wife looked perfect, but brittle—as if she'd break into pieces if you touched her. His children were never there…always in boarding school. The people who worked for him never really joked around or chatted, like normal staff. The boss wasn't even there most of the time, so we were cleaning a pristine house.'

Sadie's mouth twisted now.

'We got paid in cash. If I'd been less naive, and hadn't been so broke, I might have questioned that.'

She sat down again.

'Because I'd witnessed the murder, and could identify the victim when they showed me pictures, the police asked me if I'd be a witness if they ever caught my boss and got him into court. By now, there weren't just British detectives talking to me—there were detectives from France, Spain, America… They told me that even if I said no, I'd still be in danger. My boss would be coming after me. So I agreed to put my statement on video, so it could be used as evidence someday. And then the only way they could protect me was if I went into a witness protection programme.'

Sadie stopped talking. Her mouth was dry. Quin was just looking at her. Then he stood up and walked over to the drinks cabinet and poured himself another shot of whatever he'd poured before. He swallowed it down. He looked at her again, and held up a glass in question.

She shook her head. 'Just some water, please.'

He brought over a glass. She took a sip. Now Quin started to pace back and forth. Sadie could feel the volatile energy crackling around him...between them. Eventually he stopped and turned to face her, shaking his head.

'You've had four years to come up with a story and you couldn't come up with anything better than a plot straight out of a soap opera?'

Sadie felt deflated. And then angry.

She stood up, clutching the glass. 'I told you it was a lot.' Then she thought of something and said, 'Those nightmares I used to have—remember? They were actual memories of watching that man being murdered, except I had no idea what they were about.'

Quin's jaw was hard. 'Easy to say now...'

Sadie's hand was clutching the glass so tight her knuckles were white. 'Why do you think I didn't want to go on a date with you when you asked me out? Because I couldn't. I wasn't allowed to get close to anyone.'

Quin looked at her. 'So you're saying you only had a relationship with me because you couldn't remember that you were in a witness protection programme.'

'Exactly.' Sadie had to admit that it did sound fantastical. But that had been her reality.

Quin asked, 'When did your memory return?'

Was he starting to believe her? It didn't look like it. If anything, his expression was even more obdurate.

'The day Sol was born. That was when I remembered everything. It was as if a veil had been pulled back, revealing the past. I think going into the city sparked something... I knew instinctively that going into a city was dangerous...so much CCTV. I'd been told to move around—to stay in places big enough to get lost and not so small that I'd stand out. Sao Sebastiao was perfect.' Before Quin could say anything else she asked, 'Why do you think I had no personal effects in my apartment in Sao Sebastiao? Why was there no trace of me online?'

'What's your real name?'

Sadie's chest tightened. 'It's Lucy White...but I haven't been Lucy for years now. I'm Sadie.'

Because she'd been Sadie when she'd met Quin and had Sol that was who she was. Who she wanted to be.

'You mentioned family...where *were* your family?'

'My parents died when I was a baby—in a car crash. I was unharmed. I was adopted, and lived with a family until I was around five. But then they had problems and handed me back into care. I was brought up in foster homes after that. It's harder to get adopted the older you are.'

Sadie tried to hide the lingering pain of knowing that she hadn't been enough for her adopted parents. She'd carried that feeling of being excluded all her life, like a stubborn wound. It had only been when she'd met Quin that she'd felt as if she'd found a home.

She could see now that it was part of the reason she'd fallen so hard for him—instinctively relishing the safe harbour of his love without understanding why until after her memory returned. Her upbringing had been a far cry from Quin's.

That reminder made her feel exposed and vulnerable, she said, 'I'd lost my memory. I had no idea who I was. You did know who you were, but you kept your past from me as much as I kept mine from you.'

Quin's mouth tightened. 'You looked me up?'

Sadie nodded. 'Afterwards, yes. Primarily to see if I could find you online, so I could keep tabs on you and Sol.'

Quin sounded a shade defensive. 'I never lied to you.'

'Maybe not,' Sadie conceded, 'but I never lied to you either. Maybe I would have had to if you'd pursued me and I hadn't had the surfing accident and lost my memory.'

Quin sounded weary. 'Why don't you cut all this melodrama and tell me what really happened? You had the baby and you realised that you weren't really cut out for the domestic life so you ran. And when you realised that I'd made my fortune you came back to see what you could get out of it. Why not just admit that and save us all some time? I'd respect you more if you did.'

Quin's words landed like stinging barbs all over Sadie's skin. The hurt landed heavily in her gut. 'Because that's not what happened.'

There was only one way to prove her story. 'Can I use your computer?'

He frowned a little. 'Okay.'

Sadie loosened her grip on the glass, only realising

then how tense she was. She put it on the desk, and went around to the other side of the desk and sat in Quin's chair.

She opened up the internet search engine and searched for a name and accompanying news articles. Then she wrote a name and a number on a piece of paper, and pulled up a biography of that person. She left the tabs open and stood up.

She pointed to the screen. 'You can read news articles about the murder and the implosion of the organised crime gang that was run by the man who owned the house I worked in—the man I saw murder another man. Then you can ring the person who was my witness protection case officer. If you don't believe she's real, you can see her Scotland Yard biography, which I've also pulled up.'

She came around the desk again and stood in front of Quin.

'That's why I left that day, Quin. Because if I hadn't, and if they'd tracked me down, we'd all be dead now. The only reason I'm here at all is because all the people involved with that man and his gang—anyone who would have needed to kill me, or anyone close to me— is now dead.'

Sadie turned and walked to the door, but before she opened it she stopped and turned back.

'For what it's worth, I haven't been with anyone else since you. I wanted you to know that.'

Then she turned away again, opened the door and left.

Quin wasn't sure how long he stood looking at the door. At the empty space Sadie had left behind.

Not Sadie. Lucy.

What she'd just told him was like something from a lurid American daytime soap script. Ridiculous. A fantasy. And yet the words that reverberated in his head were, *'I haven't been with anyone else since you.'* As if that was the most important thing.

And yet he couldn't deny the frisson of satisfaction he felt at hearing that admission.

He shook his head. *Focus.*

Maybe, he thought now, *maybe she's actually mentally unwell.*

Maybe she'd created this fantasy explanation and perhaps she even believed it—because she certainly seemed genuinely invested in it. So much so that he'd doubted his own disbelief a couple of times.

What was it they said? The more elaborate the story, the more likely it was to be true, because no one could remember that amount of false detail.

Quin shook his head. No. It was nonsensical. He'd never heard such a labyrinthine story in his life.

Eventually he broke out of his stasis and went and sat down behind his desk. He looked at his computer screen and saw a slew of press headlines and images of a crime scene. Men on the ground. Dead.

Notorious crime boss living in plain sight SLAIN by his own gang!

Quin got a jolt. He'd heard of this man. He'd been a well-known billionaire businessman and philanthropist. There'd always been murky rumours about where his wealth had originated and whispers of links to criminal activity, but nothing had never been proven.

There was mention of him being on every Interpol list,

with a high reward for any information. And there was a small paragraph about an anonymous witness who had been put under protection for their own safety. A witness who could place him at the murder of Brian Carson. Another well-known criminal.

Breathless column inches described how the crime boss had lived in one of London's leafiest and most exclusive suburbs—how he'd even socialised with royalty and sent his children to the best schools in Europe. How the authorities had watched him for years but hadn't been able to pin anything on him because he'd had such a vast network of people to do his dirty work.

Lucy White. Had she really just been an innocent, naive young woman who'd unwittingly worked for a notorious criminal gang boss? Maybe she'd been part of it and had taken a deal to get out if she confessed what she knew?

Quin's head throbbed. He made a call to Claude, an old friend who worked in security. He was someone he trusted, because he had helped him stay off the grid when he'd wanted to escape the furore around his family five years ago, after it had been revealed that his 'father' wasn't his biological father. When he'd walked away from everything he'd known and taken control of his own destiny.

He greeted his friend with the minimum of niceties and gave him the details. 'Can you look into this?' he asked. 'And also Lucy White? Let me know what her involvement was, if any.'

'Sure… This is an…unusual request…is everything okay?'

Quin clamped his mouth shut, to stop himself from revealing that the mother of his child might possibly be linked to a major crime syndicate. He just said, 'Everything is fine, thanks, Claude. I owe you.'

'No problem. I'll get back to you ASAP.'

Quin terminated the conversation. He felt edgy, restless. Didn't know what to think. All he could see were Sadie's huge eyes and how innocent she'd looked. Had she even really lost her memory? But then his conscience pricked. He recalled the headaches she'd get—so painful that they'd leave her pale and sweating. And the nightmares, when she would wake, sitting bolt-upright in the bed, screaming, her body slick with perspiration, eyes huge and terrified. He remembered cradling her in his arms as she said, over and over again, *'So much blood... I've never seen so much blood.'*

She couldn't have faked that.

Or maybe she could, and he was just a supremely gullible idiot taken in by a huge pair of eyes and a lithe body.

She'd been a virgin.

He could still remember the spasm of pain that had flashed across her face as he'd breached her tight body. The way she'd resisted him before her body had softened and moulded around his, giving him the most erotic experience of his life. Blood was pumping to his groin just at the memory.

Quin surged to his feet. *No.* He would not do this— sit here and torture himself. Tomorrow he would quiz Sadie about everything and look for chinks and holes in her story, and when Claude came back with the inevitable proof that she was indeed not what she seemed Quin could wash his hands of her for good.

* * *

The following day Sadie was cleaning Sol's bathroom, going through the motions automatically, avoiding thinking about last night. She needed to keep busy. She hadn't seen Quin yet—he'd taken Sol to school that morning. She felt curiously empty. Flat. Anti-climactic. She might have expected to feel somehow more…relieved, or even happy after finally telling Quin what had happened. But clearly he had viewed her explanation with outright suspicion.

Would it change anything?

But at least she'd done it. Told him the full truth. He would have to believe her eventually.

But would he ever forgive her? Maybe in his mind even the threat of death wasn't a good enough excuse for her leaving.

All she'd known at the time was sheer terror at the prospect that she might be the cause of any harm coming to Quin or Sol. She would do the same today if she needed to.

She heard a sound nearby and turned her head to see Quin appear in the doorway, as if manifested straight out of her thoughts. He took her breath away before she could try and control her response. He was dressed in dark trousers and a shirt. Open at the neck. The casual clothes did little to hide the powerful musculature of his torso and wide shoulders.

She only realised belatedly that she was still on her knees and she stood up, very aware of her hot face and perspiration from working.

He said, 'We're going out for lunch.'

Sadie struggled to understand why he was announcing this. 'Okay… You and Lena? Or Roberto?'

After all, they were the only other people she'd met so far.

Quin frowned as if she was being dense. 'No, you and me.'

'Oh…'

Sadie's insides fluttered, but then she told herself she was being silly. Obviously he just wanted to talk to her about everything she'd landed on him the previous evening. This wasn't a date.

She said, 'We don't have to go out if you're busy.'

Maybe it would be better to talk in a private space rather than out in public.

'You haven't left this house and gardens since we arrived,' he pointed out.

Sadie hadn't even realised that. But it was true. She remembered how, when she'd been with Quin before, she'd never wanted anything much more than to be with him. In their modest beachside house. She could appreciate now that part of that must have had to do with the danger she'd known was out there, but cloaked by her faulty memory.

Quin was looking at her. 'Okay, then, that'd be nice,' she said.

'Leave the cleaning things there. Sara will be back later—she's recovered from the accident.'

Sadie took off the cleaning gloves and took a second to check her reflection. She groaned slightly. As she'd feared, a shiny face, and hair scraped back to stop it getting in her way.

She released her hair from the clip she was using to

hold it and quickly ran her fingers through it, to try and make it look a tiny bit presentable. She left the room and made her way to the front of the house, where Quin was waiting by a small, sleek sports car in the main court-yard.

Sadie came down the steps. Her chest felt suspiciously tight. 'You got your dream car.'

'I did.'

From what Sadie remembered him telling her about this particular car, it was fully electric. She reached out and touched the sinuous line of the roof. 'It's beautiful.'

'Sol loves it.'

Sadie looked at Quin, delighted by that fact. She wanted to hoover up every piece of information about her son.

Quin came around and opened the passenger door. Sadie had to contort herself slightly to get in, but the seat seemed to mould itself around her body like mem-ory foam.

Quin got in and started the engine. Sadie could barely hear it as they made their way down the driveway and out into the suburban Sao Paulo streets. She felt a bit like an alien, beamed down onto planet Earth. She'd spent so much time hiding in the shadows that she'd never luxu-riated in just being driven down a sunny street, looking at people going about their business.

Her life had been on hold and now, finally, it was be-ginning again. She was here with Quin, and whatever this was between them might be complicated and gnarly and prickly, but she was also with her son and that was the main thing.

Absurdly, emotion sprang up and made her eyes water.

Quin glanced at her at that moment and asked sharply, 'Are you okay?'

'Fine…fine,' Sadie said quickly, blinking her eyes. 'It's just the sun.'

Quin reached over and pulled down the sun visor. He said, a little gruffly, 'I didn't think to let you get your bag or things.'

Sadie shrugged. 'It's fine. I don't have much anyway.' She thought of something and said a little stiffly, because she was suddenly embarrassed, 'I'll pay you back whatever I owe you when I can.'

Quin's hands tightened marginally on the steering wheel. 'You've been cleaning the house. I shouldn't have let you do that.'

'I didn't mind,' Sadie admitted easily. 'I don't like being idle. Anyway, it's what I've been doing for the last four years, in between some hairdressing jobs, so I'm used to it.'

She felt Quin looking at her as they pulled to a stop at some traffic lights. They were getting closer to the city centre, and Sadie could feel her heartrate inevitably rise at the thought of all those people and the proliferation of CCTV cameras. She took a breath. It would take her a while not to worry about that any more.

'So how did it work, then?' Quin asked.

He sounded mildly interested, but Sadie could still hear a trace of scepticism. It hurt that he didn't trust her, but she couldn't blame him. In a way, she was lucky he hadn't just thrown her out on her ear after hearing her story.

Sadie had to consciously relax her hands, which were

clasped tightly together. 'I moved around a lot. Stayed away from big cities.'

'Aren't they easier to get lost in?'

'Surprisingly, no. There's so much CCTV. I stuck to big towns, but not cities. I took menial jobs—cleaning offices and hotels. And I'd ask busy hair salons if they needed extra help at Christmas—things like that. Places that had enough foot traffic that the customers wouldn't strike up a conversation or get to know you as a regular stylist.'

'Where did you live?'

'Hostels, mainly. Sometimes hotels, if I was lucky enough to have the funds. Sometimes I even got a short let.'

'Didn't the police give you any money?'

Sadie shook her head. 'You're expected to get a job and provide for yourself. They paid for my ticket to Brazil, and some modest funds to help me disappear, but that was it.'

'You said you weren't with anyone…?'

Sadie looked at him. Did he doubt what she'd told him? His profile was so hard.

'No one. I couldn't afford to get close to anyone.'

'Did you want to?'

Sadie shook her head. 'No, there was no one.'

How could there have been? she wanted to say to him. All she'd thought about was him and Sol, going into internet cafés when she thought it safe enough and looking Quin up online, hoping for a glimpse of her son. Hoping for a glimpse of Quin. Hoping she wouldn't see him with another woman.

Quietly, Sadie said, 'If I'd felt I had a choice, of course

I wouldn't have walked away. But I knew Sol was in good hands...you've been an amazing father.'

Quin was pulling into a valet parking area outside a building on one side of a pretty leafy street. When the car had stopped he looked at her and said, 'That's probably because I had to become mother and father overnight. I had no choice but to step up.'

Because she'd stepped out.

He didn't say it, but he obviously meant it. She was tempted to defend herself by pointing out that she hadn't had a choice either, but she said nothing. Clearly her explanation had fallen into some space between them where Quin was not ready to believe her. Yet. She couldn't necessarily blame him—it was a lot to take in.

He would have to believe her eventually, though, because there was no other explanation. But right now she couldn't imagine that even then there'd be much of a thaw in the air.

CHAPTER SEVEN

IT BECAME APPARENT as soon as they walked into the restaurant—impossibly sophisticated, with soft music playing, big open spaces and tables arranged around a central open-air pond where exotic fish swam lazily, all overlooked by a wall of green foliage—that Sadie was woefully underdressed.

It was in the raised brow of the impeccable maître d' and in the looks of the other diners as they were led to their table in a—thankfully—discreet corner. The clientele was sleek and beautiful, casual but elegant, the women in silk and linen, men in suits. By the time she was sitting down opposite Quin her face was burning with humiliation.

He glanced at her as he flicked out a linen napkin. 'What's wrong?'

'What do you think?' she hissed, wishing she could wrap her own napkin around her, to hide her tatty T-shirt. 'I'm completely out of place here. I can't believe they let me come in with you.' She added, 'If it was your intention to humiliate me then it's worked beautifully.'

Quin put his napkin down and looked around, and then at Sadie, whose face was still burning. He had the grace to look guilty. He said, with genuine contrition,

'That wasn't my intention at all. I'm not so petty. It just didn't occur to me… I should have given you time to change.'

Sadie looked at him. She believed him. Her anger fizzled out and she made a face. 'I'm not sure I have anything smart to change into, except for that dress I wore the other night, and that's not appropriate either.' She seized the moment and pointed out, 'Maybe it didn't occur to you because you're used to walking into places like this without a second thought.'

He looked at her sharply. 'What's that supposed to mean?'

'The fact is that you were born into this world. You take it for granted.' She shook her head. 'Why didn't you tell me about your family? About where you came from? You never even mentioned your brother.' She hoped the lingering hurt wasn't apparent in her voice.

He looked at her. 'You really want to talk about this now?'

'Why not?'

She'd laid herself bare last night, but Sadie held her breath, not sure if Quin would comply.

But eventually he said, 'Because I was escaping them—and that world. Being with someone who didn't know who I was with all its accompanying noise was…a novelty. I liked being anonymous.'

Sadie absorbed that. 'Why did you need to escape?'

A muscle pulsed in his jaw. He didn't look at her now. He said, 'Because I'd found out that everything I'd grown up taking for granted was a lie.'

'Do you mean about your father not being your biological father?'

He nodded. 'I only found out when we had an argument because I didn't want to go into the family empire, like my brother did. It explained why I'd always felt like an outsider in my own family. He'd tolerated me for the sake of the family reputation.'

'The articles I read said you were disinherited.'

He looked at her. Proud. 'I disinherited myself, and that's when I went to Sao Sebastiao to work on my own tech stuff.' His gaze narrowed on her. 'And then I met you.'

Back to her. Obviously his omission wasn't as big a sin as her actions.

Sadie suddenly had so many questions, and was determined not to let him change the subject, but at that moment she registered a prickling sensation at the back of her neck. Someone appeared at her shoulder. She nearly jumped out of her skin, inadvertently knocking over an empty glass with her hand.

It was only the waiter. Heart pounding, she apologised and righted the glass. She realised her hands were trembling with the sudden rush of fright and adrenalin.

The waiter poured them water and left again.

Quin was frowning. 'What was that about?'

Sadie looked at Quin, mortified. 'I'm sorry, it's just that I'm not used to sitting with my back to the people around me.'

Quin looked at Sadie. She was pale. Her hands were trembling slightly. She glanced over her shoulder again and he noticed how she let her hair fall so that her face was hidden. It was a move that had obviously become habitual.

He stood up. 'I'll switch with you.'

Sadie looked up at him, eyes wide. 'Do you mind?' Quin shook his head. She stood up and they moved around the table. She sat down in his seat. It was only when Quin sat down that he was suddenly aware that he felt a prickle of discomfort.

He suddenly recognised that very primitive instinct that must be within everyone—to feel a sense of danger at not knowing what was behind you. It did make him feel a little vulnerable...

'I'm sorry,' Sadie was saying. 'You must think I'm being ridiculous, but I've just got used to always being aware of my surroundings. I had to.'

'If what you say is true.'

The words came out before Quin had a chance to fully think them through. He registered the look of hurt on her face, but something inside him had hardened. He pushed down the urge to trust her—because if he believed her that would send his world even more off its axis.

He suspected rather uncomfortably that having to let go of the anger that had felt so righteous for so long would expose more uncomfortable things that he'd never really dealt with. Like the sheer hurt. Pain. Loss. Sense of betrayal. A betrayal made worse because his own mother had abandoned him too. It had been so much easier when Sadie had been the straightforward villain and not a potential victim.

Sadie sagged back in her chair, as if she might be feeling the weight of his thoughts. 'Why would I make such a story up?' she asked. 'It would have been easier to say that I thought I couldn't cope.'

'But not as sympathetic.'

Sadie's eyes flashed, but before she could say anything the waiter was back to take their order. Quin noted that some of the colour was back in Sadie's cheeks, and something in him eased a little. He scowled at himself. They ordered, and the waiter left again.

Quin sat back. He was prepared to indulge her for now, at least. 'So, tell me, then, how did you end up in Brazil?'

Sadie's mouth compressed for a moment, and Quin had to restrain himself from reaching across the table and touching his finger to her soft lower lip. Before, they'd touched each other all the time, and that tactility had been a revelation for him after growing up with little in the way of open affection. It had been impossible not to respond to Sadie's irrepressible nature, and the affection—physical and emotional—that she'd given so freely.

'Why should I tell you anything more when you don't believe me?'

'I'll suspend my disbelief.'

He saw how Sadie's glance flicked past him to the restaurant behind him and then back. He hated to admit it, but such a reflex could only be borne out of an ingrained habit. When they'd been together before she'd used to dislike going out to bars or restaurants, preferring to stay in and cook for them.

'I picked Brazil to come to because I couldn't think of anywhere further. I figured I could get lost in a country like this.'

'And your witness protection team just agreed?'

Sadie nodded. 'I didn't have any family or relationship ties. Once they'd furnished me with a new identity and new documents they were happy to get me out of their hair. They already had my video deposition, so if anything did happen to me it wouldn't ruin their case. They liaised with the police here, but only so far as to let them know my background. After that I was on my own. I had to find a job and support myself.'

'Why didn't the police here or back in the UK try to track you down when they didn't hear anything from you after losing your memory?'

'I found out when I contacted them after my memory returned that they *had* been trying to track me down. But my mobile phone was gone, and a lack of resources and lack of personnel meant they were limited in what they could do to find me. I hadn't been in Sao Sebastiao for long before we met, so I hadn't yet checked in, telling them my latest location. The onus on keeping myself alive and safe was really on me. They didn't have any obligation beyond being a place for me to call in case I needed help or to find out information—like how the case was going...'

Their starters arrived, and Quin forked some salad absently into his mouth as he said, 'So what happened when your memory returned?'

Sadie swallowed her food. 'I knew I had to check in with them. I had no idea what was going on. When you'd gone to the hotel for the night, after Sol's birth, I got in touch. They'd received intel that my old boss *had* actively been looking for me in North America... They couldn't be sure that he hadn't extended that search further to South America. They'd started looking for me in lists of missing people when they couldn't find me.' When Quin stayed silent, Sadie continued. 'The fact that he was actively looking for me... I knew I had no choice. I had to go.'

The waiter returned and removed their plates as Quin absorbed this. Eventually he asked, 'Why didn't you just tell me?'

'I agonised over it. That whole night. It would have been the easiest thing in the world… But I kept looking at Sol, and all I could see was how small and vulnerable he was. It wasn't just about me. It was about you and him. I couldn't take the risk of telling you, just to make myself feel better, and risk your lives as well as mine. The witness protection team had been very clear that *anyone* I got close to would be a target too.'

Quin sat up straight. 'But I could have done something… I could have taken us somewhere else—somewhere safe.'

Sadie looked at him. 'First of all, I didn't know that. I didn't know you had access to any resources. But that wouldn't have changed anything. These people have access to information that you can't even believe. They have access that goes beyond the scope of any police force. If they'd tracked me down they wouldn't have hesitated to kill you too. And Sol.'

Sadie's eyes were wide now, her face leached of colour again. It was as if she was reliving a nightmare, and Quin had to concede that, whether she was telling the truth or not, she believed her own story. Or else she should be on the stage, winning awards for her acting skills.

Hurt at this reminder that Quin hadn't confided in her while they'd been together, no matter what he'd just revealed about liking his anonymity, made her say, 'There's no point talking about it any more—not until you're prepared to accept it's what actually happened.'

With perfect timing the waiter returned with their

main courses. Sadie looked stupidly at her plate. She
hadn't even registered what she'd ordered, but apparently it had been fish, artfully arranged on the plate on
a bed of herbs, with a seasonal salad and baby potatoes.

For the next few minutes she avoided looking at Quin
and focused on her food. Even though her appetite had
fled, to some extent, she'd learnt the hard way not to skip
a hot meal if it was handed to her.

To Sadie's surprise, the tension defused a little and
they ate in silence. If not companionable, then at least
not overtly antagonistic.

She glanced up and saw Quin's muscled forearms,
exposed where he'd rolled up his sleeves. Her insides
twisted with awareness. He had big hands with long fingers. Blunt nails. Masculine.

Their plates were taken away and coffee and biscuits
delivered. Sadie took a sip of the fragrant, rich drink
and closed her eyes, appreciating the aroma. She could
feel the constant inner tension and vigilance she'd carried around for years slowly starting to unwind within
her. In spite of Quin's anger and distrust.

When she opened her eyes again Quin was study-
ing her. Her cheeks grew warm. She put her cup down.
Quin didn't look away. He'd always had that confidence.
No shyness. Not like her. He'd used to look at her in-
tently before, until she'd start laughing or try to break
his focus.

Once, when they'd been in bed, she'd asked, 'Why do
you look at me like that?'

'Like what?'

'Like you want to see all the way inside me.'

'Maybe because I do…maybe because I wonder who you really are.'

The memory made Sadie shiver a little.

'Cold?' Quin asked.

Sadie shook her head. 'No, just a memory…' Impulsively she said, 'I'm glad Sol had you.'

'He will always have me.'

There was a clear warning in Quin's tone.

Sadie looked at him. 'He also has me now. I'm not leaving again.'

The air quivered between them. But the tension was broken when Quin said, 'Come on—we've a stop to make before we pick up Sol from school.'

Sadie's heart jumped. She would get to see her son at school! She stood up and followed Quin out of the restaurant, noting how the manager practically bowed to him on the way out. A far cry from their very humble life together in the beach house in Sao Sebastiao.

Back in the luxurious confines of the car, Sadie noticed they weren't going back towards the suburb. 'Where are we going?'

'You need some clothes.'

Sadie opened her mouth and was about to protest, but nothing came out. She did need clothes. She still felt self-conscious. The restaurant had highlighted her shabbiness. No doubt Quin was wondering how on earth he'd let lust overwhelm him the other night, now he'd seen her in the harsh light of day against a sophisticated backdrop and in comparison to other women.

'I don't have money to pay you back now, but I will as soon as I get a job.'

Quin made a sound that was somewhere between a sceptical noise and *'whatever'*, which made Sadie even more determined to do what she could to get her life back on track as soon as possible. There was bound to be a hair salon looking for a stylist in the city somewhere.

Quin was slowing down now, and expertly parking in a space outside what appeared to be a very upmarket boutique, with mannequins in the window wearing long sheaths of glittering dresses.

Before Sadie could say anything, Quin was out of the car and opening her door, extending a hand to help her out. She was loath to touch him when he'd all but told her that making love to her had been a huge mistake, but there was no other way to get out of the low-slung car gracefully, so she put her hand in his and gritted her teeth against the all too predictable reaction in her blood.

She pulled away as soon as she was standing up straight, and studiously ignored Quin as he gestured for her to precede him into the boutique. Once inside, Sadie immediately wanted to turn and leave again—but she couldn't, because Quin was right behind her, saying something over her head to the very elegant manager. His Portuguese was so fast, Sadie couldn't keep up.

He pushed her gently towards the woman, who was now smiling and saying, 'Come with me, please.'

Sadie had no choice but to let herself be led into a luxuriously carpeted inner room, where there were rails of clothes—everything from jeans to evening gowns.

The woman stood back and looked Sadie up and down assessingly. Then she said, 'Okay, let me see what we have for you…'

* * *

'Her story stacks up, Quin. She is who she says she is, and it's a miracle she survived. This organised crime gang was one of the most sophisticated and deadly in the world. They signed their own death warrants, though, when Almady murdered someone in his own home. He was getting complacent…arrogant…and that led to his ultimate downfall.'

Quin was standing outside the boutique, where he had gone to take this call from his friend. A heavy weight lodged in his gut. Sadie's story was true. He would trust Claude with his life.

But not the mother of your own child? prompted a voice.

Quin pushed it aside.

Quin had told his friend that Sadie was Sol's mother. He asked, 'Is there any danger now?'

His friend sighed. 'No—and I've checked it out thoroughly, with contacts who would know. Anyone who wanted her gone is dead or disappeared now. She has no relevance any more, thankfully. But I should tell you that one of Almady's associates was in Sao Paulo just over a year ago, sniffing around, showing people her picture, so they were intent on finding her. She did the right thing, leaving.'

Quin went cold. It had come that close? The danger? 'Could I have protected her and Sol?' he asked. 'If she'd told me?'

Claude was deadly serious when he answered, 'Three moving targets are easier to find than one.'

For the first time Quin had to wonder what he would have done in Sadie's situation. The thought of harm coming to Sol—his skin went clammy. Of course he would have done whatever it took to ensure his son was safe.

Even if that meant walking away?

His friend's voice cut off that uncomfortable question.

'Quin, I can't emphasise enough how real the threat was. And she'd witnessed a murder, so she had the trauma of that on top of the trauma of being on the run. If the gang hadn't imploded the way they eventually did, who's to know if she could have ever settled down again? The fact that she lost her memory and was blissfully unaware of the danger she was in, unwittingly putting you and her baby in, is frankly a little terrifying. It's sheer luck they didn't track her down in that year.'

'I swear it could have been made just for you. I knew you'd look amazing in it.'

Sadie smiled weakly at the boutique owner—Monica. She'd already tried on an array of day wear, and the woman was so nice and friendly that Sadie hadn't had the heart to refuse when she'd said she had an evening dress for Sadie to try on.

Sadie was almost afraid to look at her reflection in the mirror, very aware that the dress was made of some kind of gold lamé and clung to her body like a second skin.

But the other woman said, 'Look at yourself, please... you are stunning.'

Sadie gave in, and for a second didn't recognise her own reflection. She'd never worn an evening dress in her life—apart from when she'd gone to that party to try and see Quin. And calling that dress an 'evening dress' had been a stretch.

But this...this was Cinderella territory.

Sadie glowed with a golden light. Her skin looked almost translucent next to the gold. The dress was simple, with two thin straps and a low-cut vee that ran between her breasts, making them look more ample than they were. It was a feat of engineering that Sadie would never be able to figure out.

It hugged her neat waist and clung to the flare of her hips, making her look far more shapely than she really was, and then fell in what could only be described as a waterfall of gold to the floor in soft, shimmering folds.

Her back was bare to the top of her buttocks.

Sadie had never been a girly girl, but this dress was evoking a multitude of things inside her. Yearnings and memories. The only other dress she'd ever had was the simple white broderie anglaise sundress she'd worn on the beach, while pregnant with Sol, when she'd married Quin.

Or, as he'd reminded her, *not* married Quin.

A sound came from behind them—a discreet cough. Monica went to the curtain and pulled it back, saying, 'Senhor Holt, please tell your girlfriend how stunning she looks.'

Girlfriend.

Sadie immediately froze. That couldn't be further from the truth of what was happening here. She was already anticipating the censorious look on Quin's face—he hadn't brought her here to play dress-up in gold lamé dresses! Maybe he'd suspect that she'd introduced herself as his girlfriend.

At the last second she reached for her neck, where her engagement ring would be hanging from the chain she'd put it on. But she let out a breath of relief when she remembered she'd left it in a drawer by the bed in the guesthouse for fear she'd lose it while cleaning.

Quin appeared in the space where Monica was holding open the curtain, blocking out all the daylight behind him with his wide shoulders, and all Sadie could do was look helplessly at him through the reflection in the mirror.

At first he was frowning, stern, but then he looked at her and his expression was wiped blank. And then... it changed. The only way Sadie could describe it was... *arrested*—as if someone had just punched him in the back. His eyes were glued to hers. And then moving up and down, taking her whole body in from bare feet to the top of her head. The look on his face was so intense... and something else...*hungry*.

Sadie's skin prickled. She had to be imagining it. He was angry, not hungry. And then his phone rang again, and he said something to Monica before turning away to take the call.

Monica came back, all business, helping Sadie out of the dress.

When Sadie went to look for the clothes she'd been wearing she couldn't find them. Monica made a face and handed her some of the new clothes, saying, 'I think these might be more comfortable for now. I'll get the rest packed up.'

Sadie took the clothes, and when she was alone again saw that there was a new pair of jeans and a loose silk shirt. A very luxe version of the casual style she liked. There was a pair of soft slip-on brogues. And—her face coloured—underwear. It was as if Quin had surmised that her underwear would be as tatty and cheap as the rest of her very limited wardrobe.

In any case, she was pretty sure he wasn't investing in new undergarments for his benefit. He'd made that clear.

When she'd changed—underwear and all—she caught her reflection in the mirror again and had to make a wry face. Even with unkempt hair and no make-up she could see that the quality of these clothes added an elegance that couldn't be manufactured any other way except by money.

She sighed. She'd never be able to afford to pay Quin back for this—an entirely new wardrobe of clothes.

She went out of the changing area into the main salon. Quin was off the phone now. He had his back to her, arms folded, looking out of the window. Legs planted wide. She could tell he was brooding from his stance.

He turned around then, and said, 'Ready?'

Monica reappeared, smiling—and no wonder. Quin had just dropped a small fortune. 'I'll have everything sent over today,' she said.

'Thank you. I appreciate it, Monica. *Adeus.*'

'*Obrigado.* Goodbye, Sadie.'

Sadie forced a smile. 'Thank you.'

At the last moment, Monica said, 'Wait!' and Sadie turned around at the door. The woman handed her a pair of sunglasses and said, 'On the house.'

Sadie smiled for real. 'Thank you,' she said, and slipped them on, appreciating the protection from the afternoon sun outside. And, more importantly, the protection from Quin's dark gaze that kept flicking to her as he manoeuvred the car out of its parking space and into the traffic.

There was silence between them. Tension was growing and becoming suffocating.

When they were stopped at some lights, Sadie blurted out, 'I never said I was your girlfriend, and I didn't ask to try that dress on. She insisted, and I didn't have the heart to say no...'

Quin looked at her. 'What?' He frowned and then he seemed to absorb what she'd said and waved a hand. 'I didn't even hear her say that.'

Sadie felt a little deflated. 'What is it, then?' she asked. 'You're tense enough to crack.'

A muscle pulsed in his jaw. The car moved forward again with a little jerk. Eventually Quin said, 'Not here. We're almost at the school. We'll talk later.'

Soon they were pulling up outside a big modern building. Small children were coming out of the gates, being greeted by parents and carers. It was a happy throng, and for a moment all Sadie could do was blink to try and keep her emotion back.

Quin must have noticed, because he took her by surprise, touching her hand in a fleeting movement. 'Okay?'

Sadie shook her head and nodded at the same time, and tried to swallow the lump in her throat. 'It's nothing. I just... I used to fantasise about this—about someday being able to collect Sol from school. A normal thing that most people take for granted with their kids.'

She didn't look at Quin, afraid of what his expression might say, so she didn't see the way he looked at her thoughtfully.

He got out of the car and came around to help her out. Sadie stood beside him and pushed the sunglasses onto her head, straining to see Sol's distinctive reddish blond hair. And then there he was—a blur of energy, colliding with his father.

'Papa! I missed you.'

And then he noticed Sadie, and took her completely by surprise.

'You came too!' he said, as he threw his arms around her waist.

Sadie's legs nearly buckled at his easy and open gesture.

He pulled back, unaware of the emotional earthquake he was causing, and looked at Quin. 'Papa, can I show Sadie my classroom?'

'Sure, let's go.'

Sol took Sadie's hand and pulled her towards the school. A woman who must be a teacher was standing talking in the doorway and Sol said, 'Miss Diaz, this is my friend Sadie. I'm showing her my classroom.'

'Okay, Sol, that's fine.'

The woman smiled at Sadie, and then seemed to do a double take when she saw her similarity with Sol. Sadie pretended she hadn't noticed.

Quin stayed behind, talking to the teacher, and Sadie savoured every second with her son, chattering nineteen to the dozen as he showed her where he sat, where his locker was, and where he put his shoes and which artwork was his.

When they got back to the house Sol was despatched to change out of his school clothes and Sadie finally met Sara the housekeeper—a friendly, no-nonsense woman. Roberto had left snacks, and when Quin disappeared to his home office to make some calls Sadie sat with Sol and ate them, helping him with the little piece of homework he'd brought home.

She was so engrossed that at first she didn't notice

when Quin arrived back into the main living area. He'd changed into board shorts and a T-shirt. He looked like the man she'd first met, and her heart flipped over in her chest.

She realised then that he was looking at her with a strange expression—as if he'd never seen her before, or as if she was about to do something outrageous.

His gaze went to Sol. He said, 'Enough books—let's get outside and play some football.'

Sol was outside like a shot.

Quin looked at Sadie. 'Are you coming?'

The way he said that, so easily, made something cave inside her. Some of the wall she'd erected to protect herself in the last few years. It had been the only way she could survive.

'Okay,' Sadie said quickly, and tried to hide how pathetically seismic it felt to be invited to play with her son.

She stood up.

'I'll just change into something a bit more casual.'

When she went down to the guesthouse she found Sara putting away the new clothes that must have just been delivered.

Mortified, she protested, 'Please, don't. I can put them away myself.'

The woman smiled. 'It's no problem…it's almost done.'

Sadie sat on the bed when Sara was gone and looked into the dressing room, now full of brand-new clothes. And then she noticed something hanging at the back… a glimmer of…gold.

She got up and went into the room, reaching for the glimmer, sucking in a breath when she pulled out the stunning gold dress. It slid through her fingers like liquid. It must be a mistake. Sadie made a note to let Quin know. She had no doubt a dress like that must have cost a fortune. Even she recognised the designer's name, and she'd been more or less living under a rock for the last half a decade.

There was a shout from outside and Sadie went through to the main living area to see a red-faced Sol, standing in the door with mud streaked across his legs.

'What's taking you so long?'

The dress was forgotten as a surge of emotion gripped Sadie, bright and pure. But she managed to get out a strangled-sounding, 'Nothing…give me one minute.'

CHAPTER EIGHT

Quin couldn't focus on the game. He missed another pass from Sol, who groaned. But Quin's vision was filled with a pair of long, shapely pale legs, expertly dribbling the ball to the goal, followed in hot pursuit by Sol.

Sadie was wearing short denim shorts and a loose T-shirt, which she'd not long before carelessly tied up into a knot at her waist, revealing the smooth skin of her back and lower belly. Her hair was pulled up into a messy knot, tendrils escaping. No make-up, just a sweaty face.

Something in Quin's chest ached, and he absently put his hand there, as if he could soothe it. He realised that in this moment Sadie looked more or less exactly as he remembered her when they'd first met. But that had been before she'd walked away from him and her newborn son and all the good memories had become toxic.

And yet…as much as he'd love to cling on to that outrage and anger, as he had for the last few years, cultivating it like a cold, hard diamond in his chest, he knew he couldn't. Not now that he *knew*. Not now that his friend had told him Sadie had had nothing to do with the gang. She'd been an unwitting bystander, caught in the crossfire. Living on the run to stay safe. To stay alive.

Quin still couldn't quite grasp the full significance of what that had meant for her.

At that moment the ball landed at his feet, but before he could react Sadie was hurtling towards him and colliding with him full force, driving him backwards.

He landed with an *oof*, and with Sadie still welded to his body, because he'd automatically put his arms around her. There wasn't a point where they didn't touch. Thigh to thigh, hip to hip, chest to chest. And also, as Sadie drew her head back slowly, breathing harshly, practically mouth to mouth.

'I'm sorry,' she gasped. 'I thought you were going to move.'

But Quin hardly heard her. All he could see were those blue-green eyes. His son's eyes.

A rogue thought popped into his head: if they had another child, would it too inherit her eyes? The thought was so unexpected that Quin felt a little winded.

And then, predictably, a certain part of his anatomy started responding to Sadie's proximity.

Her eyes widened and her cheeks went pink. She said, 'I thought you said…' She trailed off.

'I said it wouldn't happen again,' Quin gritted out. 'Not that I didn't want it to.'

'Are you gonna kiss Sadie, Papa?'

They both turned their heads at that moment, to see Sol crouching down beside them, watching with open curiosity.

He said, 'If you want to, it's okay. I've seen Maria's papa kissing her mom.'

Immediately Quin stiffened and put his hands on Sadie's arms, to push her up and away from him as he said, 'No, I am not going to kiss Sadie. We just fell, that's all.'

Sadie scrambled to her feet and Quin could see the red of her cheeks, even though he wasn't looking straight at her. This was exactly what he wanted to avoid—confusing Sol. Although Sol had already started kicking the ball again, oblivious to the tension in the air and, it would seem, to any confusion.

Quin opened his mouth to say something, but at that moment Roberto called out from the house.

'Dinner is ready.'

Sadie said, 'I'll just wash my hands first.' And she fled towards the guesthouse.

Quin had to curb the urge to follow her and—

And what? asked a voice. *Punish her for turning you on so easily by making love to her? After telling her it wouldn't happen again?*

Thoroughly flustered, frustrated, and feeling as if the ground was shifting underneath him, Quin went straight to his own room to freshen up—starting with a very cold shower.

Sadie was still trembling under the shower spray a couple of minutes later. Trembling from the way Quin's body had felt underneath her. All hard sinew and steel and muscle and beating heart, thumping unsteadily against her chest. She'd wanted to put her head down, put her ear close to that strong beat. As she'd used to when they'd lain in bed.

Before.

And then she'd felt another part of his anatomy stirring against her, and any thoughts of listening to his heart had melted in a flash of heat. To her shame, she'd even forgotten that Sol was there, watching them. Until he'd spoken.

Quin had moved so fast to push her off him that her head was still spinning.

He did still want her. But he didn't want to want her. Well, he'd made that clear the first time they'd made love. Disappearing like a thief in the night.

Sadie turned off the spray and stepped out of the shower, drying herself briskly and putting a towel around her head and another around her body. She went into the dressing room, but instead of gravitating towards the jeans and shirts, she found herself moving to the dresses and pulling out an olive-green silk shirt dress with a slim gold belt.

She let the towel drop and pulled on some of the new underwear—wispy pieces of silk and lace that felt far too flimsy and decadent. Frivolous… It had been a long time since she'd felt frivolous.

But she couldn't deny that here in this place, when she was with her son at last and had told Quin the truth of what had happened, she felt lighter. Buoyant. Hopeful. In spite of the ever-present undercurrents.

She towel-dried her hair, leaving it in damp waves, and then slipped on the dress and a pair of flat sandals. She made her way up to the main house. The early evening air was warm and balmy.

When she went inside Quin and Sol were already sitting at the table.

Sol saw her and jumped up. 'You sit here, Sadie, beside me.'

Sadie's heart spasmed. She smiled and sat down, and

only then risked a glance at Quin, whom she fully expected to be looking stern. But he wasn't. He was looking at her with that half-arrested expression again. Like the one he'd had when he'd seen her in that dress in the shop. Which reminded her…

She said, 'They sent over that gold evening dress with the other clothes from the boutique. It must be a mistake. I'll pack it up so it can be sent back.'

Quin shook his head. 'Leave it…it's fine.'

Sadie would have protested, but Sol had started chattering as he spooned some of the delicious pasta into his mouth, and Quin reminded him not to talk with his mouth full.

Sadie let the incredibly soothing chatter of her son wash over her, making the appropriate responses when he looked at her with those wide eyes, pasta sauce around his mouth. Without thinking she took a napkin and dipped it in a glass of water, before using it to wipe his face.

Sol merrily went back to eating. Sadie looked up and saw Quin staring at her. She immediately felt self-conscious—she hadn't even considered that maybe she didn't have a right to touch Sol as a mother would, without thinking. But when she looked at Quin again it was as if she'd imagined it. He was smiling at Sol indulgently and her heart turned over again. She remembered that expression because he'd looked at her like that.

Before.

When they'd finished eating, Quin stood up and said to Sol, 'Bath time and bed.'

The little boy's lower lip protruded almost comically,

but Sadie could see that the day's activities had worn him out.

He got up and followed his father, but then stopped and came back to Sadie. 'I had fun today. Will you play with me again tomorrow?'

Sadie smiled. 'I'd really like that.'

Then Quin spoke. 'Can you wait for me to put Sol to bed? I want to talk to you.'

A quiver of tension lanced Sadie's belly. 'Sure,' she answered, feigning nonchalance.

Quin and Sol disappeared. But before Sadie could start clearing the table Sara came in and said, 'Make yourself at home in the lounge, Miss Ryan. Would you like tea or coffee?'

'No, thank you—and please call me Sadie.'

The woman smiled and got on, clearing the table with brisk efficiency.

Feeling a little redundant now that she didn't have anything to occupy her time or justify her existence here—because being a mother to her son was still an unspoken quantity—Sadie did as she was bade and made her way into the lounge. A room she hadn't spent much time in at all.

She surveyed it now. The soft, comfortable furnishings were very elegant, but not intimidating. She could see scuffs and marks on the furniture. Children's books on the lowest shelves that made up one wall. All signs that a child lived here.

She crouched down and picked out one of the books. It was a classic that even she remembered: *Guess How Much I Love You*.

She sat down and flicked through the pages, and her

vision blurred a little as she looked at the pictures and followed the story, thinking helplessly of the amount of times she'd lain in a lonely bed somewhere and wished with all her heart that Sol and Quin could feel the love she had for them.

'I would have thought you're a little above that reading level.'

Sadie tensed and looked up, blinking rapidly. She'd got lost in the story. She forced a smile. 'This was one of my favourites. It's a classic.'

'Yes, it is. Sol loved it.'

Sadie bit her lip in case she blurted out her sad story of sending them both her love from afar for all those years.

She got up and put the book back and faced Quin. He was obviously determined to ignore the electrical current that sprang into action whenever they were close. She would do her best to ignore it too. Even though she couldn't help but be aware of his tall, lean body encased in low-slung denim jeans and a short-sleeved polo shirt.

Again, he reminded her of the surfer boy tech nerd she'd first met. But then, he'd never actually been either of those things. She had to remember that and use it as a shield. He'd never fully trusted her.

She said, 'You wanted to talk?'

Quin went over to a cupboard that Sadie realised was a drinks cabinet when he pulled back a sliding door.

He looked at her. 'Drink?'

Sadie felt she might need some sustenance for whatever it was Quin wanted to talk about. 'Sure—whatever you're having.'

'I'm having whisky.'

'I'll have a little. Maybe I'm developing a taste for it.'

Quin poured her a drink, and then one for himself, and brought over two crystal tumblers, handing her one.

'I've watered it down.'

'Thank you.' Sadie accepted the glass and took a sip. It didn't taste as strong as it had last night. It trickled down into her stomach and sent out a warming glow.

Quin faced her, and after a moment said baldly, 'I know you're telling the truth.'

Something bubbled up inside Sadie: relief.

Quin went on. 'I spoke to a friend of mine. He owns a security company and I asked him to verify what you told me.'

The bubble of relief burst. So Quin hadn't come to believe she was telling the truth because he trusted her. He'd had her story verified. But she'd more or less instructed him to do that, so she shouldn't really be feeling hurt.

'What did he tell you?' she asked, as if there wasn't a great gaping chasm opening up in her chest.

'He confirmed what you told me. He told me the gang were notoriously dangerous. He told me that you were an unfortunate victim, in the wrong place at the wrong time. He also told me that one of them appeared in Sao Paulo as recently as last year.'

Sadie could almost feel the blood rushing out of her head before dizziness took hold.

Quin was by her side in a second, taking her arm and saying, 'Sit down.' He cursed softly as she did so, and said, 'I shouldn't have told you that.'

Sadie had gone cold all over at the thought of one of those odious men here. So close to Quin and Sol in spite of everything she'd done. Her huge sacrifice. Her hand gripped the glass.

Quin crouched beside her. 'Take a sip of your drink.'

He took the glass out of her hand and held it to her mouth. Sadie obediently opened her lips and let him pour some of the alcohol into her mouth. Her eyes watered a little, but the drink revived her.

Quin put the glass on a table and she looked at him. 'Now can you see? They were actually here! Looking for me! What if they'd found out who you were? Everything I'd done would have been for nothing—'

'Claude has assured me that there were no links to me or Sol. We weren't officially married, and Sol was registered with my name when he was born.'

'Yes, of course. Thank God...' breathed Sadie. Then she asked, 'Did your friend say if there was still any danger? The detectives in London told me that every threat was gone, but I feel like I can't ever fully relax.'

Quin moved back to sit on the edge of a couch, near the chair. Their knees were almost touching. Sadie ached to reach for Quin and climb onto his lap. Just have him hold her, tightly, making her feel nothing could harm her, as he used to, before her memory had returned and she'd run... The more she thought about it now the surer she was that she must have known of the threat in some dim recess of her damaged memory and she'd relished his ability to make her feel safe. But inevitably their close contact would lead to far more incendiary things than feeling safe...

'Claude has assured me that anyone who would have wanted to see you...' Quin faltered.

'It's okay,' Sadie said. 'You can say it. See me *gone*. I lived with it for four years.'

His jaw clenched. The fact that he was obviously having trouble saying it out loud—that she could have been killed—provided her with some level of vindication. But it was small.

Quin went on. 'He assured me there's no threat, but I've asked him to make absolutely sure of that. He'll let me know if he finds anything.'

'Thank you,' said Sadie.

For the first time in four years she had someone else who knew. Who cared. Except Quin didn't care about her…

She shook her head. 'You don't have to do that—it must be costing a fortune.'

Quin stood up and moved towards one of the windows, hands in his pockets. He turned back and his mouth was quirked up slightly. That tiny hint of lightness was enough to take Sadie's breath away.

He said, 'Yes, Claude is expensive, but he's thorough.' Then the quirk in his mouth disappeared. He was serious. 'There's no way I won't make sure that you're safe. You're Sol's mother. He's lost you once. I won't let that happen again.'

Emotion was back, swelling inside Sadie's chest. She fought it down, not wanting Quin to see how vulnerable she felt. 'Thank you…for saying that. After losing my own parents and spending so much time in foster care, the last thing I would want is to put Sol through losing me again.'

Quin turned and faced her fully. 'You said you were adopted after your parents died?'

Sadie nodded. 'Until I was five. But then the marriage broke down, and neither one could afford to keep me, so they sent me back into care. I was in foster homes until I left school.'

'How was that?'

Sadie looked at Quin and then quickly looked away again. She felt exposed. 'It wasn't ideal… No matter how nice the families were, it was always very apparent that I didn't belong to them. They were mostly kind, though. I was one of the lucky ones. Some foster kids have much worse experiences than me.'

'"*Mostly* kind"?'

Sadie repressed a shiver. 'There was one home… where the son was a few years older than me. He came into my room one night but his mother caught him. I was moved within a week.'

'Sadie…'

She looked up and saw that Quin was pale.

'You were almost—'

'Nothing happened,' she said quickly, trying to forget about that moment when the teenager had been looming over her in her bed. She could still remember the terror robbing her of her voice. She took another sip of her drink to try and calm herself.

Quin asked, 'After everything you'd experienced, weren't you tempted to take Sol with you when you left?'

Sadie put down the glass and stood up too. The traumatic memory of those days after giving birth was never too far away. She'd been so exhausted, and full of raging hormones and instincts—chief of which were to clamp her baby to her chest and never let him go.

'Of *course* I wanted to take him—it went against everything in my body to leave him behind. But then I remembered watching that man execute someone right in front of me. As if it was nothing. The easiest thing in the world. The man was begging for his life and my boss just…shot him. I knew that if he ever found me a baby would be nothing to him. No deterrent. That's what stopped me from taking him. And knowing that he would be with you. I trusted you, Quin. I knew you'd be a good father.'

And I loved you. I still love you.

She didn't say those words, even though they were high in her chest, begging to spill out. She would always love this man—even like this, when things had changed so irrevocably between them. But she knew he wouldn't appreciate hearing it now. Maybe never.

'I knew you'd be a good father.'

The way Sadie had just said that with such conviction, as if there had never been any doubt in her mind… It robbed Quin of breath for a moment. She'd already told him she thought he was a good father, but this was different. She'd not hesitated to leave their days-old baby with him, and he was only fully appreciating the significance of that now.

Up until he'd held tiny Sol in his arms he'd not really understood how on earth he could be a father, not having experienced that bond with his own. He hadn't shared his fears with Sadie, too ashamed to admit that he might not be able to do it.

But as soon as the soft, vulnerable weight of his son had been handed to him his knees had almost buckled with the weight of love and awe slamming into him.

He'd made a vow to love and protect his child with every atom of his being.

The fact that she must have felt that too, and yet she'd walked away from her baby, made Quin say now, 'I haven't acknowledged how hard it must have been for you.'

She looked at him from across the room, and even now, in the midst of this conversation, he was supremely aware of how strong her pull was. She'd changed for dinner into a silk shirt dress, and all evening he'd been aware of the way the belt encircled her narrow waist. Of the buttons, open to the point where he could just make out the shadow of her cleavage. He'd imagined her breasts encased in silk and lace…felt his body responding against his will.

He could still feel the weight of her body on his when they'd collided earlier. The press of her breasts against him. Her breath on his mouth. He'd *ached* for her. For four years…

She was shaking her head now, and saying with tell-tale huskiness, 'It was the hardest thing I've ever done.'

Quin resisted the effect her voice had on him. 'It's a lot to take in. To undo four years of suspecting you'd just walked out on a selfish whim.'

Sadie let out a surprised sound, halfway between a laugh and a sob. She put a hand to her mouth and then took it down again. Shaking her head, she said, 'It couldn't have been further from "a selfish whim". There were so many moments when I almost turned around and came back, telling myself that one more day wouldn't hurt. All I wanted to do was confide in you, have you tell me it would be okay…but I knew that was selfish and potentially fatal.'

Quin had a sensation that he was free-falling into a massive void with nothing to hold on to. There was no escaping it now, he could no longer cling to the anger and the rage that had felt so justifiable for so long. In the absence of any explanation. Now he *knew*. But, if anything, it didn't seem to make things feel clearer or easier—things felt more complicated.

You loved her and she hurt you in the worst way possible. She walked out on you just like your mother did.

He *had* loved her. Much as he might have tried to deny it since her return. He'd loved her more than he'd believed it possible to love another human being. But that love was gone. And even though she might have had very compelling reasons for leaving him and Sol, he knew he would never be able to trust her enough to revive those feelings. Falling for her had shown him how vulnerable he still was, and he'd vowed never to allow himself to be vulnerable like that again.

The attraction that had driven him to her the other night…the attraction he still felt…was borne out of frustration and anger. But surely that volatile mix would lose its potency now that he had all the facts?

Because the thought of allowing himself to cleave so fully to Sadie again was…frankly terrifying. And she was looking at him now as if she could see all the way into his head. He had to push her back, establish boundaries, find a path forward so they could co-exist and parent their son.

Before he could say another word, though, Sadie was

speaking. 'It's been a long day and I'm tired. I think I'll say goodnight.'

Immediately Quin felt remorse. What was it about this woman that scrambled his brain so effectively?

'Of course. We can talk again about where we go from here.'

She looked about as eager for that conversation as he was. She just nodded and left, and Quin watched her slim, pale legs through the window as she walked down the garden. She cut a lonely figure, and he couldn't help but think of the life she'd lived—essentially on her own, always.

He could empathise. Even though he'd grown up within a family, he'd always felt somehow apart. He'd had no mother and a distant father who hadn't been his father at all. A brother who had been invested in taking over the family business. He couldn't even blame his brother, because they'd never really been encouraged to bond.

Quin had to curb the very strong urge to follow Sadie. *And do what?* asked a voice. *Make love to her again and muddy the waters even more?*

Quin turned away from the view of Sadie disappearing into the trees. No. The attraction would fade. He needed to put down boundaries but he also needed to think about the best way to move forward while incorporating Sadie into their lives.

Sadie had had to leave quickly. The air between her and Quin after that conversation had been taut with tension and a million swirling things. The attraction she'd felt, and the need for him to touch her and take her into his

arms, had been so overwhelming that she'd been terrified he'd see it on her face, or she'd blurt something out…

She'd not really felt tired when she'd used that as an
excuse to leave, but a wave of weariness moved through
her now. It had been a tumultuous twenty-four hours.

Clearly it was going to take time for Quin to absorb all
this. She could understand that. She'd had four years to
deal with it every day and she still couldn't quite believe
what she'd had to do, or how she'd had to live.

But hopefully, after tonight, they could leave the past
behind and start to move on. To where, Sadie had no idea.
But as long as she got to be a mother to her son—that
was the most important thing.

Yet when she went to sleep that night, her dreams were
filled with images of her and Quin at the beach house.
And when she woke the next morning her cheeks were
damp from shed tears and her heart was sore.

'I have to go to San Francisco tomorrow, for a conference
where I'm a keynote speaker. I'm taking Sol and Lena—
she has a daughter there, so it's an opportunity for her
to pay her a visit too. You're welcome to come with us.'

Sadie looked across the lunch table at Quin. It was the
weekend, and Sol was outside kicking a football around
with some friends who had come to play. She'd been enjoying the banal domesticity of it all after the intensity
of the previous day and evening, but now her insides
clenched a little.

She couldn't read Quin's expression. Did he want her
to come? After all that had transpired?

'I don't mind staying behind if you want to have some
time with Sol on your own.'

As much as she would have loved to suggest leaving Sol here so she could look after him, she knew that would be a step too far, too soon.

'Actually,' he said, 'I have a favour to ask.'

Sadie blinked. She could do something for Quin?

'Of course. What is it?'

He made a face. 'There's a social event that I have to host. I set up a charity foundation a few years ago, to help kids from disadvantaged backgrounds get scholarships into tech courses. But every year the speculation about my relationship status, or lack thereof, overshadows the work of the charity. I could do with a date.'

Sadie blinked again. 'You're asking me to be your date?'

Her silly heartrate went up a notch.

'If you don't mind?'

Sadie was confused. 'But… I thought I'd be the last person you'd want to be associated with?'

'There's a little more to it… I think we need to tell Sol who you are. He's already growing attached to you, and he'll start to get confused. I thought it might do no harm for us to be seen in public together. We can put out a statement saying that you are Sol's mother, and then we can suggest at a later date that our brief reunion is over. But by then it'll be established that you are Sol's mother, and hopefully the story will die a quick death in the social columns.'

This was almost too much for Sadie to take in. She stood up from the lunch table and started to pace back and forth. She tried to articulate her tangled thoughts.

'So…we'll appear in public? Pretending we're together?'

She looked at Quin and he nodded.

'But what will we say when they ask where I've been?'

Quin shrugged lightly. 'As little as possible. We won't suggest that you haven't been in Sol's life…we'll keep it vague. If anyone looks you up they won't find much—just like we didn't when we looked you up after you lost your memory. I've been largely off the social scene's radar, living here in Sao Paulo, so for all they know you could have been here all the time—just not with me.'

So, Sol would know who she was… That made Sadie's heart expand with a mixture of joy and trepidation. What if he didn't like the idea of her being his mother? And what about the other stuff? Appearing in public as Quin's girlfriend? Lover? Partner? Only to be excised 'at a later date'…

But could she really complain? As he said, this would establish her as Sol's mother. It would put her firmly in his life. If not Quin's life.

It would be easy for Quin to keep Sadie at a distance. But he wasn't doing that. He was giving her a chance to step into their world and take her place there. This was huge.

She looked at him. He was sitting back in his chair, long legs spread under the table, one arm across the back of the chair beside him. Supremely relaxed. As if he wasn't wielding a high level of control over her life like some kind of a puppeteer.

He frowned a little as he registered her lack of response and leaned forward, taking his arm down. 'I thought this would be what you wanted?'

Sadie clasped her hands. 'It *is*. I want Sol to know who I am—and thank you for that… I want everyone to know. But it's just a little daunting…the thought of being thrust centre-stage after four years of being anonymous and living in the shadows.' She shook her head. 'I've dreamt of this moment for so long… I thought it might never come. But now it's here it's just a little overwhelming.'

An expression Sadie couldn't decipher crossed Quin's face, and then he said a little sheepishly, 'I'm sorry. I didn't really take all that fully into consideration. If you'd prefer to wait until another time—?'

'No,' Sadie said quickly, terrified of letting this moment slip out of her grasp. 'I've spent four years in purgatory. I can do this.'

CHAPTER NINE

'*I'VE SPENT FOUR YEARS in purgatory. I can do this.*'

Quin hadn't been able to get those words out of his head for the last twenty-four hours because they'd resonated inside him, touching too many chords. He'd been in purgatory too but he had to admit that he hadn't fully appreciated how daunting it would be for Sadie to step out in public as Sol's mother.

His purgatory had been that of not knowing why she had left. The purgatory of her betrayal. But he knew now that it hadn't been a betrayal. It had been the absolute opposite, in fact, of what he'd experienced with his own mother.

His mother's act had been selfish. Cruel.

Sadie hadn't been cruel or selfish. She'd sacrificed her own happiness and risked her life to protect them.

His anger at her might be gone, but Quin couldn't deny that the memory of the pain was still there. Like scar tissue. Warning him to be careful. Not to be susceptible again. Because all he wanted now was to be able to co-exist with Sadie. To have her in their lives, but not in Quin's gut any more. Making him feel…too many conflicting things. Making him *want*—

No. He shut that down.

All he needed was for equilibrium to return. Sanity. So he could start living his life again, perhaps even take a lover—as he'd planned to do the evening Sadie had appeared before him like a genie out of a bottle. Bringing the past with her. A past that he could finally start to move on from.

That's why he knew this was a good idea, bringing her front and centre into his life, publicly. It was the most expeditious way of establishing their relationship and her as Sol's mother, even as they both knew that it was just a façade.

She would also have to get used to a certain level of public interest as the mother of Quin Holt's son. There was no getting away from his family legacy.

Then, when the time was right, they'd announce their amicable break-up and could then get on with independent lives, co-parenting their son.

Quin watched Sadie across the aisle of the plane, where she sat with Sol, their strawberry blonde heads close together. Sol was looking at a book and pointing things out to Sadie, who was smiling.

They'd planned on telling Sol last night about her identity, but he'd been so exhausted after playing with his friends that he'd practically face-planted into his dinner.

Sadie had hidden it, but Quin had noticed her disappointment.

He checked his watch. They had at least another six hours' flying time. They'd stopped for a short refuelling break in New York.

Quin said, 'Sol?'

His son looked up. 'Yes, Papa?'

Quin's heart turned over at his son's open trust and

love. He held out a hand. 'Come here. I want to tell you something.'

Sol put the book aside and jumped off the seat. He came over to Quin, who pulled him up between his legs. Sadie looked at Quin and he sent her a nod of his head. She went pale, but nodded back. She understood.

Quin looked at his son. 'You know how you were asking about your mother a while ago, and I said she'd had to go away?'

Sol nodded, looking serious.

'Well, when I said Sadie was a colleague from work, it was not really true.'

Sol frowned. 'Did you tell a lie?'

Quin nodded. 'I did. And I know that's wrong, but I did it because it was too big a secret to tell you straight away.'

'What secret?'

'That Sadie is your mother.'

Sadie was holding her breath so hard that she had to force herself to breathe. Her heart was thumping. Her eyes were glued to Sol, who looked over at her now, suddenly shy, cleaving closer to his Papa. Her heart ached.

He looked up at Quin. 'Sadie is my mom?'

Quin nodded. 'Yes she is.'

'But where was she?'

Quin looked at her. 'I think you should ask your mother that question.'

Sadie got off her seat and went over to kneel down near Sol. 'Sol…?'

The little boy looked at her warily. She mentally sent up a prayer for forgiveness and understanding.

She said, 'When you were born, I had to leave. Someday I'll explain why I had to go, but I really, *really*, didn't want to go. Leaving you was the most horrible thing I've ever had to do. And for the last four years I've been on a really long journey to come back to you.'

Sol's eyes widened again. 'Like a magical adventure?'

Sadie felt like smiling sadly. She nodded. 'Something like that.'

'That's cool.'

Sadie couldn't help smiling at her son's interpretation of her absence as some kind of epic adventure. He was too young to feel the more adult emotions of anger and betrayal. Like his father.

Sadie continued. 'What's most important for you to know is that I won't ever be leaving again, and even if I'm not living in your house with you I'll be somewhere very close. I promise.'

'You can stay with us—can't she, Papa?' Sol looked up at his father.

'We'll have to see. Sadie might want her own space.'

'But she has the garden house by the pool.'

'Don't worry. No matter what happens, you'll still see her as much as you want.'

Sol looked as if he was going to say something else, but he actually said, 'Okay, Papa. Can I watch a movie now?'

'Yes—in the bedroom, in your pyjamas. You need to sleep before we land.'

'Okay, Papa, I'll change.'

Sol sped off, seemingly not all that fazed by the momentous news he'd just received.

Lena appeared. 'I'll get him changed and washed and settled.'

'Thanks, Lena.' Quin smiled at her.

Sadie got up off her knees and sat back down on the seat. She felt a little dazed. Winded. Now her son knew who she was.

She looked at Quin. 'Do you think he took that in?'

Quin nodded. 'He's processing the information. He can bring stuff up from a year ago as if it happened yesterday. It's just how they do it at that age.'

'I hope he's not upset.'

Quin shook his head. 'He's not upset.'

Sadie's emotions were suddenly surging upwards and bubbling too close to the surface. She stood up and mumbled something, then fled to the bathroom, locking the door behind her just as the emotions erupted out of her with a huge sob. She couldn't breathe or see. Everything was blurry.

'Sadie, open the door.'

Quin. She'd thought the knocking on the door was her heart.

There was no hope of her regaining control. Reluctantly she opened the door, and then Quin was in the small space and she was enveloped in his arms—the safe harbour she'd longed for every night for the past four years.

Sadie wasn't sure how long she cried and how long he held her—it could have been minutes or hours. When she finally pulled back from Quin's chest all she could see was a massive damp patch. Mortified, she said, 'I'm so sorry—'

'It's fine.'

Quin's voice had a rough quality. She was afraid to look at him, but he tipped up her chin with a finger and she had no choice. She was sure her face and eyes must be swollen and blotchy, but remarkably she felt better. At peace. Lighter.

'Thank you,' she said huskily.

Quin's gaze moved to her mouth, and even in the aftermath of her emotional storm Sadie could feel her blood spike with heat. Mortifying… He couldn't have made it clearer that he would not touch her again, but she was too weak right now to pull back.

'For what?' he asked.

'For telling Sol… For not casting me away on sight as you had every right to do.'

Quin rubbed his thumbs across her cheeks, wiping her tears. 'I'm sorry that I'm only realising now how hard it must have been for you, and how strong you've had to be to get through the last four years.'

Sadie's heart hitched. 'And for you too.'

A moment quivered between them, delicate and fragile. For the first time since she'd come back into his life Quin wasn't looking at her with that mixture of distrust and antipathy. It was something altogether…*warmer*.

Sadie looked at his mouth. She desperately wanted him to kiss her… Even as she had that thought his head started to lower towards hers—just as a sound came from behind Quin, and then a voice.

It was Lena. 'Sorry to interrupt, but Sol is asking for Sadie to watch the movie with him.'

Quin stopped moving. His eyes met Sadie's. She trembled with the heated intent she saw there. It didn't mean he'd act on it. She needed to be strong. To protect herself and not let him see how much she ached for him.

Quin spoke. 'Okay, she'll be right there.'

He took his hands down and stepped back out of the cubicle. The moment was gone.

Sadie forced a watery smile. 'I'll just freshen up.'

Quin left her, closing the door behind him. Sadie heard his and Lena's voices fading as they walked away. She turned around and looked at herself in the mirror—and gasped. Her cheeks were bright pink, with traces of her tears in salty tracks. Her eyes were overbright, and still a bit bloodshot from crying. Hair in total disarray. And here she was thinking he'd looked at her with desire. She was delusional.

No. She was in love, and aching for something that had been lost for ever.

Sadie groaned softly and turned on the tap. She had to try and minimise the damage of her overflowing emotions. She would just have to hug the thought of how good it had felt to be held in Quin's arms again close to her, like a guilty secret.

A couple of hours later, Quin pushed open the bedroom door on the plane. The light was dim. A tablet lay on the bedcovers, upon which lay his son and Sadie.

Sol was curled into Sadie and her arm was around him. They'd fallen asleep.

He could still hear her gut-wrenching sobs and feel the racking shudders through her slim body as he'd held her in his arms. No one could manufacture that kind of raw emotion.

Quin felt grim. He now knew—had known in that moment when he'd almost kissed her—that in spite of all the revelations and the tangle of emotions in his gut—each one screaming at him to not let her get too close—that the thought of not touching her ever again was simply not an option.

He'd been ready to make love to her back in that bathroom, and probably would have if they hadn't been interrupted. Their attraction was undeniable. Unavoidable. Clearly the hope that it would fade after the truth had come out had been futile. A fantasy.

So it would have to be allowed to run its course—because only then would Quin finally be able to put Sadie to one side so they could all get on with their lives. Together but apart. He had his son. He didn't need anything more.

Sadie looked at the clothes that had already been hung up by some invisible person in the hotel suite's dressing room. They'd arrived a couple of hours before, and were now in one of San Francisco's most exclusive hotels, with views that stretched all the way to the Golden Gate Bridge from the terrace that wrapped around this penthouse suite.

Sadie had a bedroom to herself, as did Quin and Lena. Sol was in a room that connected with Lena's. There was a kitchen and a dining room. A media room and a gym. And a lap pool outside, heated. The sheer scale of the opulence was breathtaking.

She spied something familiar hanging up and reached for it, pulling out the gold evening dress. Had Sara packed this under instruction from Quin? For the event he had mentioned? Just the thought of wearing it made her feel self-conscious. But then she imagined Quin look-ing at her the way he had in the boutique—

There was a light knock on her door and she whirled around to see the object of her thoughts standing in the doorway. He was wearing a suit, no tie.

'Sorry to disturb you.'

She shook her head. 'You're not disturbing me.'

Things had felt stilted and formal between them since she'd been woken by Quin on the plane some hours ago. She'd still felt very mussed-up and a little fuzzy after her crying jag. He, on the other hand, had looked pris-tine. He'd obviously showered and changed into this suit.

She asked, 'Are you going out?'

They'd had a light lunch when they'd arrived, and Lena had gone out to do some shopping. Sol was in the living room, reading comics.

Quin nodded. 'I have a meeting at my office.'

'Do you need me to look after Sol?'

'If you don't mind… Lena should be back soon, in any case, and she's going to take Sol with her later this af-ternoon to her daughter's place. They'll stay there over-night. Lena has a grandson around Sol's age, and they've met before and like each other.'

Sadie felt simultaneously thrilled at the thought of being allowed to stay with Sol on her own, and also a little bereft at the thought of him leaving for the night.

'Oh, okay… Well, you don't need to worry about me. I can amuse myself. You must have meetings and things planned.'

Silly to feel somehow excluded, but for Sadie it touched on that very old wound of never feeling she'd belonged to anyone or anywhere. The man in front of her was the only one who had ever made her feel a sense of *home* and *belonging* and she had no right to ask that of him again.

He said, 'That event I mentioned…it's actually this evening.'

Sadie's hand tightened on the dress—she hadn't even realised she was still holding it. She let go.

'This evening?' Her heartrate sped up a couple of notches.

He nodded. 'Is that okay?'

'I…guess.'

Trepidation filled her belly. Why had she agreed to this?

She gestured to the dress. 'Sara packed this. I'm not sure it'll be appropriate, but it's the only evening gown here.'

Sadie stopped talking, afraid Quin might think she was fishing for more new clothes or something.

But Quin just said, 'The gold dress will be perfect. Lena will help you get ready before she leaves with Sol. I'll see you later. Feel free to explore and do whatever you like when Lena comes back…use the pool, or head into the city.'

Quin had left before Sadie could formulate a response. She went out through the French doors to the terrace and looked out over the city. For so long she'd seen cities as malevolent places, full of dangers, but now she would have to get used to letting all that go. It was exhilarating and terrifying all at once.

She turned away from the view. But for now she had her son to look after, and she was going to savour every moment she had with him like this. Because she had no idea what the future with him would look like once this period of pretending to be *with* Quin was over.

A few hours later, Lena's daughter Beatriz stood back and said, 'You look like a million dollars, Sadie.'

Beatriz had come to pick up Lena and Sol, and had been roped into turning into a stylist for Sadie. She was about Sadie's age, and disarmingly friendly and sweet. Sadie had had no choice but to let herself be swept along on her wave of enthusiasm.

And then a much smaller voice—Sol's—said, 'Wow, you look so pretty.'

Sadie forced a smile. She didn't see what they seemed to see in the mirror. She saw a stranger, wearing a dress that was far too revealing and far too...*gold*. She looked as if someone had poured a bucket of it over her head and it had fallen over her body, covering only strategic bits.

One aspect she didn't need help with was her hair, but Beatriz had suggested leaving it loose, saying, 'We're in California. I think casual is more suitable—and your hair is gorgeous.'

Her skin looked milk-white next to the gold.

'Now, what about this ring around your neck? I think you should wear it on your finger.'

Sadie had completely forgotten about the engagement-wedding ring. She touched it now, just as the small hairs went up all over her body. She realised Quin was in the doorway of the dressing room, dressed in a black tux-edo. How long had he been there?

She barely noticed Beatriz and Lena melting away, taking Sol with them. He was looking at her neck, where she was now clutching the ring.

'You still have it?'

'Of course I have it.'

I wear it every day.

'Why is it around your neck?'

Sadie swallowed. 'I wasn't sure how you'd feel if you saw me still wearing it.'

His eyes met hers. 'It's just a ring.'

Sadie shook her head, everything in her resisting that provocative implication that it was nothing remarkable.

Memories swamped her of how Quin had got down on one knee and presented it to her, saying, 'It reminded me of your eyes...but if you don't like it you can choose another one.'

Sadie had shaken her head, tears blurring her vision. 'No, this is perfect.'

'No,' she said now, a little defiantly, 'it's not just a ring. I wear it every day.'

She unlocked the chain and the ring fell into her hand. She put it back on her finger, where Quin had put it all those years ago. She wasn't going to let him diminish the significance of the ring that had bound them.

Quin said nothing, but Sadie could see a slash of colour in his cheeks. Eventually he said, 'If you're ready to go, my driver is waiting.'

Sadie lifted her chin. 'I'm ready.'

She wasn't ready at all, but she felt a little more empowered now that the ring was back on her finger. Quin mightn't like the reminder that he'd once professed to love her, but that was his problem.

The ring kept catching Quin's attention, twinkling in his peripheral vision. Mocking him. When he hadn't seen it on Sadie's hand since they'd met again, he'd been surprised at the sense of disappointment he'd felt. He'd seen it as an added layer of betrayal. But she *had* kept it, and worn it every day.

This further evidence of her innocence made him feel a little unmoored. Exposed.

He could recall how the ring had caught his eye in the window of a jewellery shop in Sao Sebastiao one day. Its blue and green stones. Emeralds and sapphires. He'd immediately thought of Sadie's eyes.

In spite of the gems being real, it wasn't a sophisticated ring. It certainly wasn't the kind of ring that he would ever have presented to a woman from his old social peer group. It hadn't come with an iconic name like Cartier or Tiffany.

He'd also realised in that moment that he had never really articulated the fact that he wanted to marry her— even though obviously he saw his future with Sadie, and not just because of the baby on the way. For ever. To create a family. A home. A life. For the first time, with her, he'd had a sense that that might be possible for him. The kind of life he saw people living every day but hadn't ever experienced himself.

He'd told her he loved her. He'd told her that way back—before she'd even got pregnant. The words had flowed out of his mouth as if it was the easiest thing to say in the world—when in fact he'd never said it to anyone else. It was as if when he'd met Sadie she'd unlocked something inside him. A need to be loved and love in return that he'd pushed down. Ignored. Because first his mother had abandoned him and then his father had turned his back, treating him with a disregard that had only made sense once Quin had found out he wasn't even his natural-born son.

But it had been easy to say to Sadie…and necessary.

And she'd looked at him and smiled and said, 'I love you too,' as if it was the most obvious thing in the world. As if she'd had no idea what a gift she'd just given him. Accepting him so unconditionally.

So he'd proposed to her with the ring. He'd offered to change it if she didn't like it, but she'd told him it was perfect.

And then she'd looked at him, concerned. 'Can you afford this?'

Not for the first time he'd felt his conscience prick hard—because he hadn't ever told her about his family history. He'd known he would have to one day but, shamefully, he hadn't wanted to risk her looking at him differently. Especially not at that moment.

He'd liked the person he was with her. Anonymous. No ties, no toxic family baggage, and so he'd just said, 'Don't worry about the cost. I used some savings.'

That moment when Sadie had accepted his proposal had been one of the happiest moments of his life. Happiness. He'd never truly understood that emotion until he'd experienced it with her.

Quin had waited for something terrible to happen—because he'd grown up in a world where emotions weren't permitted, where awful things happened—abandonment and emotional neglect. But nothing awful had happened and he'd forgotten about the danger. Until the day she'd disappeared. Then all the declarations of love and their promises to be together for ever had curdled in his gut, turning to acid and then to ice.

But the ice was in danger of melting now. Had been as soon as Sadie had said, just a short while before, *'I wear it every day'*, and slipped the ring back on her finger with something almost like defiance.

That moment had almost eclipsed the dress—the dress that made her look like she'd been dipped in liquid gold. But now, here in the back of his car, with a mere foot between them, the ring could no longer eclipse the dress.

Her scent—delicate, but with undertones of something potently sexy—permeated the air around them. The dress clung to every curve and dip. Cut down low between her breasts. Baring her back and the vulnerable length of her spine.

Quin had never seen Sadie like this because when they'd been together they'd lived a very simple life. No social engagements. Certainly not ones like this, where the paparazzi lay in wait. He could see them now, up ahead, cameras flashing as various celebrities and VIPs emerged from their cars, as they were about to do.

As if following Quin's line of thought, Sadie turned to him, her hair falling around her shoulders in soft waves. She wore hardly any make-up, but she *glowed* and her eyes looked huge, her lashes so long. But her mouth was tense. It made Quin's fingers itch to touch it…make it lose that line.

When she spoke, she sounded nervous. 'Quin, I've never been to anything like this in my life… I only got as far as meeting you at that party in New York. I don't know what to do.'

A surge of protectiveness rose up in him before he could stop it. He said gruffly, 'Just follow my lead. Stay in the car until I come and get you.'

The car came to a stop. Quin got out and opened Sadie's door, putting out his hand.

He saw her reluctance, but he said, 'It'll be fine—trust me.'

She looked up at him and he saw the way her expression had gone blank, as if she was retreating somewhere inside herself. As her hand met his, he wondered if this was what she'd had to do for four years. Hide behind a mask as well as a fake identity.

She stood up and they walked towards the steps that led up into one of San Francisco's oldest and most iconic buildings, where the exclusive charity event was being hosted.

As soon as the paps realised who he was, they went into a frenzy.

'Hey, Quin! Over here...'

'Who's your date? Quin!'

Sadie was gripping his hand so tightly her nails were digging into the back of his hand, but Quin just smiled and stopped for some photos. He looked down and saw Sadie's dazed expression.

He extricated his hand from hers and put an arm around her waist. She looked up. He said, 'Relax...they can't touch you.'

She smiled weakly. 'This situation is literally my worst nightmare...nowhere to hide.'

He shook his head. 'There's no more hiding.'

He knew that the statement he and his team had prepared, stating that Sadie was the mother of his child and that they were reunited, would be dropping just about now, to coincide with their appearance together tonight.

And a sense of satisfaction that he didn't want to investigate too closely rolled through him.

Sadie felt giddy, but she put it down to the sparkling wine that had fizzed up her nose and down her throat. She gazed around in awe at the decadent surroundings of one of San Francisco's most gilded buildings. She needn't have worried about her dress standing out. With all the gold on the walls and muraled ceilings, she positively faded into the background.

Quin hadn't let her go—either keeping an arm around her waist or holding her hand. She relished the contact, greedily and guiltily soaking it up, knowing it was only for appearances. He'd told her about the statement now being released, revealing her identity as Sol's mother.

Maybe her giddiness was also due not only to Quin's proximity, but to the fact that her past on the run was well and truly behind her. She couldn't be more visible now. People were looking at her and whispering, but Sadie couldn't care less. She felt safe beside Quin.

There was a steady stream of acolytes wanting to speak with Quin, and Sadie couldn't help but feel proud of all that he had achieved—even if he hadn't come from an impoverished background like her, as she'd imagined. He'd turned his back on a vast inheritance and that had taken guts.

After a little while, Quin took two fresh glasses of wine from a waiter's tray and led her out to a fragrant outdoor terrace. Sadie took one of the drinks and breathed in the evening air. The city skyline twinkled in the distance…it was magical.

'Thank you.' She raised her glass at him before taking a sip. He loosened his bow tie a little. 'You don't like dressing up?' Sadie observed.

Quin made a face. 'Not really. I never did.'

Sadie put her back to the wall and looked up at him, her gaze taking in the hard, lean planes of his face. Her conscience pricked. He looked so much less carefree than he had when she'd known him before. Was that her fault?

She pushed aside the ever-present guilt and asked, 'Were you ever going to tell me about the world you'd been born into?'

Quin glanced at her, clearly reluctant, as he was whenever his past or his family was mentioned. But eventually he said, 'Of course. I would have had to—we were having a child together.'

'I know you said you liked the anonymity, but why was it so important for you to keep your background from me?'

'I liked the version of me that you saw. Someone who didn't have a massive legacy. I'd grown up with everyone knowing who I was. Looking and judging and whispering. It was a novelty to be free of all that. You weren't tainted with any of the toxicity.'

Sadie absorbed this. 'Your brother…he's older?'

Quin nodded. He turned away from the view and rested back against the wall of the terrace, like Sadie. She turned side on to face him. The rest of the party had faded way into the background. There was only her and him.

'Primo… He was born first, hence his name. Our mother was Brazilian. There's no ambiguity about *his* paternal lineage, he resembles our—*his*—father, albeit just physically. He's a much better man. He has integrity.'

Sadie frowned. 'There are other brothers? Sisters?'

Quin shook his head. 'No, our mother had three miscarriages after Primo—that's why I'm called Quinto. Number five.'

Sadie thought of something. 'That's why you were so insistent on me going to a big hospital for the birth, isn't it?'

Quin nodded, looking slightly uncomfortable. 'I hadn't thought about it like that, but maybe it was a subconscious fear of what might happen.'

Sadie was filled with compassion. 'So many miscarriages... That must have been traumatic for your mother. Are you in touch with her?'

Quin let out a sound that was meant to be a laugh but sounded more like a snarl. 'No, we're not close. I haven't seen her since the day she left us when I was a toddler. Needless to say I don't remember much about her.'

The words landed inside Sadie, softly at first, but as she registered their meaning they detonated inside her like little bombs. She put a hand to her mouth and Quin looked at her. She took her hand down.

'I had no idea...that she walked out on you...and then...' Sadie stopped. It was too huge, the meaning of this. She turned around to face the view, seeing nothing but the enormity of what Quin had just revealed about himself.

She shook her head. Her insides were collapsing in on themselves, her guts twisting with remorse and regret.

She looked at Quin, eyes stinging, and whispered, 'I had no idea... How could I?'

'Would it have changed things? If you'd known that you were repeating the betrayal of my mother?'

Sadie shook her head. 'Please don't say that...it wasn't the same. If I'd known... It would have made it so much harder, but I wouldn't have wanted you to torture yourself, thinking that I'd done it for any other reason than out of—'

'Don't say it!' Quin said harshly.

He shook his head, tension emanating from his tall, powerful body. Sadie could feel it.

He said tautly, 'I can acknowledge that what happened with you was different...but it didn't feel different to me. All I could think about was the fact that my son was going to experience the very same act of betrayal as me. I thought that I'd somehow caused it to happen, made history repeat itself.'

Sadie's throat ached with the effort to hold back her emotion. She knew he wouldn't appreciate it. 'Of course that's not true, Quin. It wasn't your fault at all. I'm so sorry... Please believe I never wanted to betray you and Sol. It was an act to protect you.'

Because I loved you.

But he wouldn't want to hear that. Not yet. Maybe not ever.

The moment hung between them. Tense. Fraught. And then Quin's shoulders dropped.

He said, 'My mother never returned. You did. There's that, at least.'

'I came back the minute I knew it was safe to do so. And I'm not leaving ever again. I know you might not believe me yet. But hopefully you will one day.'

CHAPTER TEN

QUIN LOOKED AT SADIE. Her eyes shone with emotion and a plea. For him to trust her. To believe her. But a weight was lodged in his chest. He had accepted that she was telling the truth about the past, but he knew that he still couldn't fully trust that one day she wouldn't just leave again.

The trauma of her disappearance, compounded by the fact that his mother had done it too, was just too huge to forget—even if their motivations had been very different.

He felt exposed. He hadn't ever fully admitted to himself that he'd blamed himself on some level for Sadie's disappearance. As if he'd brought it on himself, as a kind of punishment for believing himself worthy of love. Worthy of a normal life. Worthy of not being abandoned.

And she was looking at him now as if she could read every exposing thought in his head. Thoughts that led directly to the weight in his chest, making it feel heavier and tighter.

He said abruptly, 'We should go back inside. I need to give my speech.' And then, even though every instinct in him warned him to push Sadie back, he found himself reaching for her hand and keeping her close by his side and it had nothing to do with projecting a united front for the sake of appearances...

For the rest of the evening Sadie's head reeled with the revelation of Quin's mother's actions. He didn't seem remotely inclined to forgive her, and Sadie could understand why, but she knew better than anyone that things weren't always what they seemed.

Quin had given a passionate and articulate speech about the need for everyone to have access to tech education. Sadie couldn't help feeling proud of his work to extend a hand to those who hadn't had his advantages.

After they'd dined and listened to other speeches from the charity directors, who had then auctioned off various lots, they'd been asked to move into the ballroom, where a band were playing soft jazz. Now people were starting to dance. The lights were dim, candles flickering, sending out a golden glow that made everyone look even more beautiful. Women's dresses shimmered, jewels blinging. Sadie had never witnessed such a glamorous scene.

'Shall we?'

Sadie looked down and saw Quin's hand extended towards her. Her insides plummeted.

She looked at him. 'I can't dance, Quin.'

He took her hand. 'There's nothing to it. Just follow my lead.'

She tried to resist but he was an unstoppable force, and before she knew it they were on the dance floor and he was swinging her into his chest, one arm firm behind her back, fingers splayed across her bare skin. It was enough to distract her from the fact that they were moving—largely propelled by him.

She was pressed against him, and all she could feel was the whipcord strength in his body. She wanted to close her eyes and revel in this moment, but what he'd told her kept whirling in her head, making her chest ache.

She looked up. 'Quin—'

He took her hand in his and put a finger to her mouth. 'Is this about what we spoke of earlier?'

She nodded.

He said, 'I don't want to talk of the past any more. What I'm interested in is the present moment.'

Sadie's heart skipped a beat. He took his hand away. He arched a brow in question.

Sadie half shrugged, half nodded. 'Okay. The present.'

Maybe he was finally ready to move on with a view to the future?

But then he tugged her even closer, and Sadie's cheeks flamed when she felt the burgeoning press of his very *present* arousal.

Their gazes locked. Sadie couldn't have looked away even if she'd wanted to. She felt utterly exposed, bared in her desire for him, but he was equally exposed.

He said, 'I want you, Sadie.'

There was nothing she could do except say, 'I want you too.'

'Clearly we have unfinished business.'

'We have a child—that's the definition of unfinished business,' Sadie observed, even as her heart thumped.

What did Quin mean? Was he saying that—?

'I'm not talking about that. I'm talking about *this*.'

Quin's head lowered to hers, and there on the dance floor he kissed her—a long, slow, drugging kiss that left Sadie's head spinning when he finally drew back.

Yes, resounded in Sadie's head. He was saying he wanted her and he wasn't going to fight it.

Reluctantly she opened her eyes and all she could see was the heated intent in Quin's expression, his face stark.

He said, 'Let's get out of here?'

Sadie nodded, even though she wasn't sure if her legs would function properly. But somehow they did.

Quin didn't even stop to speak to anyone. He had a tight hold on Sadie's hand and all she could do was try to keep up with his long-legged pace. She lifted the folds of the dress in one hand as they went down the steps to where Quin's driver was waiting, holding the car door open.

The journey back to the hotel was swift. Quin didn't let go of her hand all the way up to the suite, and the air vibrated between them with an electrical charge.

Once inside the vast empty suite, Sadie took her hand from Quin's. He was undoing his bow tie fully and pulling it off. He looked a little wild, and every cell in Sadie's body clamoured for her to throw herself at this man right now.

She forced herself to say, 'Are you sure this is a good idea?'

She couldn't bear it if Quin went cold with her again after making love, as if he was punishing himself, and her, for being weak.

He came towards her, all dark, heated intensity. 'Like I said, we have unfinished business. We can't move forward until we've got this desire out of our systems.'

Something inside Sadie cracked a little at the hint of desperation she heard in his voice. Her heart. He believed this was finite—or at the very least he obviously hoped it was finite. And maybe it would be for him. But not for her. She knew that.

But she also knew she didn't have the strength to resist Quin. Not when he was looking at her as if she was the only thing in the world right now. And not when she craved his touch so badly. For four years she'd been in the desert, living a physically and emotionally barren existence. She needed him now. He and Sol were bringing her back to life, restoring her faith in humanity and her sense of home. Because no matter what happened with Quin, Sol would always be her home.

But some small, self-preserving part of her made her ask, 'What if we can't get it out of our systems?'

'I believe we will. It's just lust. Chemistry.'

There it was: the confirmation that Quin didn't want anything more. Didn't expect anything more.

She felt like pointing out that four years and his hatred for her hadn't killed their chemistry. But she didn't say that. She gave in. Succumbed.

'I want you, Quin. Make love to me.'

He came close and surprised her by taking her head in his hands and tipping it up. He looked at her for a long moment, as if learning her face, and Sadie's heart was beating so fast she thought it had to be audible. She'd expected him to take her straight to the bedroom, but if he was going to be like this…he would kill her before they even got there.

'Quin,' she said weakly. 'Kiss me, please.'

He took his time, until Sadie was quivering with need—so much that by the time his mouth covered hers a shudder of pure pleasure went through her whole body. She wound her arms around his neck, opening herself up to him, and his hands splayed across her bare back, hauling her closer.

Sadie wasn't sure how long had passed by the time they'd pulled apart again. Her blood was on fire, her vision was blurry, and she was gasping for oxygen.

Quin lifted her against his chest and walked down the corridor to his bedroom. Low lamps sent out pools of light.

He put her down and Sadie had to lock her knees to stay standing. He stripped with an efficiency that she knew she didn't possess right now and stood before her, tall and powerful. Proud. Virile. She drank him in greedily, stretching out a hand to touch him, tracing over his muscles and blunt nipples, making his breath harsher.

Then he was at her feet, and Sadie put her hands on his shoulders for balance as he removed her high heels, before running his hands up her legs under the dress until he got to her underwear. He tugged it down, and she stepped out of the flimsy lacy briefs.

But Quin didn't get up. He looked up at her and pushed her dress up her legs. He caught one leg behind her knee, lifting it so that it draped over his shoulder. He kept her steady when she would have fallen at the explicit intent in his gaze.

He drew her to him with a firm hold on her waist and bottom. Then he found where she was so exposed— literally—and put his mouth to her, tasting her desire for him...the desire that beat between her legs, hot and urgent.

Sadie gasped when she felt his tongue against her, exploring, licking its way into her and finding that cluster of nerves that throbbed with exquisite pleasure. He reached up and tugged down one strap of the dress, so it fell, exposing her breast. He palmed her flesh, finding her nipple and trapping it between his fingers.

That was all it took to make Sadie fly so high that she couldn't speak or breathe or think. She could only stand in Quin's embrace as she shattered against his mouth.

Quin was drowning in Sadie's scent and taste. He'd dreamed of this on long nights when he'd wake filled with frustration and a kind of pain he never wanted to experience again.

He stood and gathered Sadie into his arms, feeling a rush of emotion that he ruthlessly pushed down. Not emotion. Just sex.

He put her on the bed and looked at her. The dress was like a golden fountain around her body. Her hair was loose and wild. Mouth swollen from his kisses. Cheeks flushed. One breast was exposed, its nipple hard, making his mouth water all over again.

He would never get enough of this woman.

The assertion slid into his head before he could stop it or refute it. But he was too wound up to care right now.

He came down over Sadie, hiking the dress up over her waist, exposing her to his gaze. He pulled down the other strap to expose both breasts and lay beside her, using his hands and mouth to make her ready again, because he knew he wouldn't last long.

She was panting, legs moving, her hands finding every piece of skin she could touch on his body, finding where he was so hard and wrapping her hand around him.

Quin reluctantly took his mouth from her plump flesh, where the hard tip of her nipple was an incitement never to stop feasting on her, but she was going to send him over the edge before he'd even found the bliss he was craving between her legs.

He moved over her and she took her hand off his flesh. With one smooth thrust he was seated inside her, all the way to the hilt, and it was an exquisite torture to exert all the control he had to move in and out and not explode on contact, to eke out the pleasure until their skin was slick with perspiration and Sadie's nails were clawing his back like a hungry cat. But finally he gave in to the gathering storm, letting it wash them both away...

Sadie wasn't sure how long they lay entwined, but she savoured every moment. Quin's big powerful body was in hers, on hers, crushing her. It was a beautiful crush as their hearts finally returned to regular rhythms.

Quin seemed as loathe to break the embrace as she was, only moving after long minutes. Sadie winced a little, but it wasn't from pain—it was from breaking the contact.

Quin lay on his back beside her. The silence was only punctuated by the sounds of sirens, distant and far below, and their breathing. Sadie turned her head to look at Quin and took in his noble profile. It made her think of something.

She pulled the sheet up to her chest and turned on her side. 'Do you know who your real father is?'

Quin said nothing for a long time, and his eyes were closed, so Sadie assumed he must be asleep.

But then he said, 'No. I'd have to ask my mother, and I have no intention of pursuing any contact with her. The rumour mill has it that he was either the pool boy or her personal trainer.'

Sadie's heart clenched for him. She knew he wouldn't want to hear it, but she said, 'She had a lot of miscarriages... she might have been traumatised.'

Quin opened his eyes and turned his head to her. 'Not so traumatised that she didn't seek solace in the arms of another man. Under her husband's nose.' Quin let out a harsh laugh. 'God knows, he was no saint either, and he pretty much abandoned us emotionally, but at least he didn't actually leave.'

'I'm just saying that perhaps things aren't so black and white. Do you even know where she is?'

Quin shrugged. 'Primo mentioned something a while back about her being in Italy with a new husband.'

'Are you close to him?'

'Probably closer than most brothers in our situation. It helped that I never had any desire to go into the family business. We never had to compete. I think he respects what I've achieved on my own.'

'So is he in touch with your mother?'

'No, but I think their paths have crossed at an event.'

'It must have been so confusing and devastating when she left...'

'Yes, it was.'

His meaning was clear: Sadie should know that because she'd done exactly the same thing. Except...she hadn't.

Emotion made her voice thick. 'If I'd known... I can't believe that I re-enacted the worst thing that ever happened to you...and did it to Sol...'

Sadie half expected Quin to get up and leave, but he

rolled towards her and put a finger over her lips. He said, 'No more talk of the past. Like I said, all I'm interested in is the present.'

He covered her mouth with his, pulled the sheet down and lifted her bodily, so that she lay on top of him. Sadie weakly gave in to his desire to push the past back, but she knew that they'd never really move on unless Quin realised that it was still casting a toxic shadow over the present—and their future.

They stayed a few more days in San Francisco, while Quin was at his conference. Lena spent a lot of time with her daughter, so Sadie got to spend more time with Sol alone. They went to the zoo and to parks. And they went to the cinema on the third afternoon—the last day of Quin's conference—to see a charming and heartwarming animated movie about dogs, which had Sol asking Sadie if she thought they might be able to get a dog.

She'd smiled wryly and told Sol that *that* question would have to go to his father.

Sol had sighed dramatically and said, 'It was worth a shot.'

It was only when they were walking back out of the cinema that Sadie noticed the shaven-headed man in dark jeans and a utilitarian-type jacket who was hovering nearby. She'd noticed him earlier that day, and she had a sudden terrifying suspicion that he'd been at the zoo the previous day.

Sadie took Sol's hand and tried not to let him see how panicked she was. She walked away from the cinema quickly and moved down a side street, then ducked into a bookshop.

'Cool,' said Sol, pulling away. 'Can I look for a new comic?'

Sadie said yes, keeping an eye on Sol in the children's section as she pulled out her phone with trembling hands. She dialled Quin's mobile and he answered straight away.

'Is everything okay?'

Sadie was trying to put her back against a bookshelf, so she could see outside the shop, and her insides lique-fied with fear when she saw the same man standing at the corner, staring straight at her. He looked terrifying.

'No, it's not. We're being followed by a man.'

Sadie's head was spinning with the implications of this. The police had been wrong. There *was* someone still out to get her—and to get anyone—

'Sadie! *Sadie!*'

Quin's voice broke through the panic but she could hardly get her words out because fear was strangling her. 'Did you hear what I said? We're being followed. The man is looking at me right now.'

'Okay, I'm sending you a photo. Please look at it and tell me if it's the man.'

Somehow Quin's calm voice managed to bring Sadie back from the brink of full-blown panic. She took her phone down from her ear as a photo pinged onto her screen. A photo of the man she'd just been looking at.

She frowned and lifted the phone to her ear again. 'Yes, that's him. But how do you—?'

'He's Security, he's been hired by me.'

'I… Oh.'

Quin said, 'Look, you don't have to worry, okay?

He's meant to be there. I have to go now, but I'll talk to you later.'

And then he was gone.

Sadie and Sol got back to the hotel a couple of hours later and she did her best to stay calm during his bedtime routine. He went out like a light, clearly happy and exhausted, but Sadie took little comfort in that.

By the time Quin arrived back to the suite she was keyed up and practically pacing the floor.

He came into the living area and stopped when he saw her. He frowned. 'Is everything okay? Where's Sol?'

Sadie stopped pacing and said tightly, 'He's fine. He's in bed, asleep.'

'So what's wrong?'

Sadie looked at him and folded her arms over her chest, as if that might hide the sense of hurt and betrayal she'd felt since talking to him earlier.

'I know you don't trust me, but I didn't think you would actually hire someone to make sure I don't disappear again, this time with Sol.'

He looked at her as if she'd grown two heads. 'What gave you that idea?'

Sadie unlocked her arms and flung out a hand. 'The man who looks like he's come straight out of Central Casting for Scary Guy. The kind of man I've had nightmares about for the last four years.'

Quin shook his head. 'He's a bodyguard—highly recommended by Claude, my friend who works in security.'

'To protect Sol from…me? In case I try to take him?'

'No!' Quin slashed a hand through the air. 'To protect you *and* Sol. Claude has assured me that you're safe from any threat, but I didn't want to take any chances—

especially since we've now appeared in the press and your face is out there.'

Sadie sat down on a chair behind her, her legs giving way.

She felt like saying, *You can say that again*. She'd nearly passed out with shock when she'd seen her face staring back at her from the front page of a daily newspaper with the lurid headline: *Quin Holt's baby mama! Who is Sadie Ryan?*

She looked at Quin, feeling a little chastened. 'I'm sorry... When I saw him and realised he was following us, I got such a fright. Then, when you said he was Security, I just assumed...' She trailed off. She'd assumed the worst. That Quin was protecting his son—from her.

'No,' Quin refuted. '*I'm* sorry. I should have told you. I meant to earlier, but I...forgot.'

Sadie's face grew hot as she thought of that morning, when Quin had stolen out of her bed as dawn was breaking, leaving her in a sated slumber. He hadn't wanted to risk Sol waking and looking for him.

They hadn't spent a night apart since making love after the charity function. Gravitating towards each other without saying a word. Making love with an intensity that left Sadie breathless and trembling but hungry for more.

It hadn't been like this before. Back then there'd been a lazy indulgence to their lovemaking; they hadn't known they were on borrowed time. But now it was as if they were up against a ticking clock that Sadie couldn't see. The ticking clock of Quin's desire for her.

'Have you eaten?' he asked.

Sadie shook her head. 'No, but I made Sol a burger.'

She hadn't had the appetite, too wound up after what had happened.

'Come into the kitchen. I'll make something.'

Sadie's mouth fell open. 'You? Make something?' It had been a running joke between them that Quin couldn't navigate his way around a kitchen.

He looked sheepish. 'Yes, me. Let's just say I've had to cultivate some rudimentary culinary skills since Sol was born.'

Sadie stood up and followed Quin into the small kitchen. She sat on a high stool and watched with interest as he took out some eggs and an array of other items, proceeding to chop and whisk with enviable skill for someone who four years ago hadn't been able to boil an egg.

Sadie remarked, 'I just assumed you'd had an indulgent mother.'

'Not an indulgent mother—just an army of staff. I don't think I ever stepped foot inside the kitchen in any of our houses.'

Curious, Sadie asked, 'Has your father—?' She broke off. 'I keep referring to him as your father...what is your relationship with him now?'

She saw tension come into Quin's body even as he said lightly, 'As minimal as possible. It's not as if he was ever a hands-on father anyway. He treated me and my brother more like staff, and his relationship with me was strained because even before it was confirmed he'd always suspected I wasn't his.'

'So he hasn't met Sol, then?'

'No interest.'

'Poor Sol...no grandparents to speak of.'

Something hissed in the pan on the stove, breaking the moment, and Quin attended to it.

When he turned back, he shook his head. 'You had no one.'

Hearing him acknowledge that fact, Sadie felt something deep inside her—a part of her that had always felt jagged—suddenly wasn't so sharp. 'Like I said, others had it much worse than me.'

'You're a survivor.'

Sadie blinked. No one had ever said that to her before.

She shook her head. 'Really, I don't think I am. I just dealt with the circumstances I found myself in.'

'Your first instinct today was to protect Sol.'

'Of course,' she breathed. 'He's the most important thing.'

'Yes, he is.'

They looked at each other for a long moment, and then Quin seemed to break out of a trance.

'Let's eat.'

He plated up a delicious fluffy omelette and some bread. He opened a bottle of white wine and they sat and ate and drank in a companionable silence that Sadie didn't want to risk by opening her mouth again.

Quin was the first to speak when he'd cleared the plates. 'Sol has a half-term break next week. After we've dropped Lena back to Sao Paulo, I was thinking of taking him to Sao Sebastiao for a few days.'

'Sao Sebastiao…?'

Sadie wasn't even aware she'd spoken out loud. It was the most cherished place to her, but also a place of heartbreak, because that was where she'd left Quin and Sol behind.

'You still go there?' she asked.

Quin nodded, suddenly looking a little guarded. He took a sip of wine and put the glass back down. Sadie felt a little confused. Surely after what had happened the place would have bad connotations for Quin? Or...

Her insides shrank as something else occurred to her.

Perhaps it was no hardship for Quin to return precisely because it *didn't* hold any emotional pain for him. Because when she'd left he'd realised that he hadn't really loved her at all? To Sadie's mind, that suddenly seemed all too plausible.

'You're welcome to join us, of course,' he said.

Sadie thought of going back to where she'd been so happy and where she'd been so heartbroken. Bittersweet... If it wasn't a chance to spend more precious time with Sol she'd almost be tempted to decline, but of course she wouldn't.

She couldn't help feeling a sense of disquiet, though, that the place where they'd been so happy would ultimately make them again...or break them.

She forced a smile. 'I'd love to come.'

CHAPTER ELEVEN

SAO SEBASTIAO WAS exactly as Sadie remembered, its buildings with their colonial era architecture spread out between the mountains and the ocean. It was all at once sleepy and beachy, but also busy. This was why she'd got off a bus here one day—because she'd deemed it the perfect place to hide out for a bit.

Little had she known how her life would change here.

They'd arrived at a private airfield shortly before, and now Quin was driving a slightly battered open-top four-wheel drive, with their luggage in the back.

Sol was jumping up and down on the back seat with excitement. 'Can I go straight over to Joao's house when we get there?'

Quin glanced at his son through the rearview mirror. 'After you unpack and show Sadie around.'

'Okay, Papa.'

Sadie smiled and looked back at Sol from where she sat in the passenger seat. She was enjoying the salty sea breeze in her hair and the sun on her skin. 'Who is Joao?'

'My best friend. He lives right along the beach—practically next door.'

Sadie had absorbed the word *beach*, but never thought for a second that Sol was talking about—

But now they were turning down a road towards a beach that looked all too familiar.

Except Sadie could see changes. There was a high fence now, where there hadn't been a fence before.

Quin was turning the vehicle towards a set of discreet gates that almost disappeared into the lush foliage.

He pressed a button on a key chain and the gates opened. Sadie held her breath as he drove onto a short driveway that opened out into an open space where a simple beach house stood. The faint sound of crashing waves could be heard in the distance.

The house had been extended, she could see that—to the sides and to the roof. But it was unmistakably the same beach house where she'd lived with Quin. Except he'd only been renting it at that time…

Sol was already out of the car and running towards a woman who'd appeared in the main doorway and was hugging him with great affection.

Sadie got out, feeling a sense of déjà vu, and slightly dizzy.

Quin met her at the front of the car and said, 'Come and meet Fernanda. She and her sister take care of the house and gardens when we're not here, and they stock up when we come.'

Sadie couldn't move, though. She just looked at him. 'It's the house. Our house.'

Quin's jaw was tight, and then he said, 'I bought it and did some renovations.'

Sadie wanted to ask *why*, but the young woman was coming towards them now, holding out her hand.

'You must be Sadie. It's nice to meet you. I'm Fernanda.'

Sadie smiled at the friendly woman, who was very

pretty, with dark brown eyes and crazy corkscrew curls in a soft halo around her head. Sadie couldn't help but respond to her easy warmth even in the midst of her shock, and smiled back, shaking her hand.

After greeting Quin with warm and easy affection, the woman led them in, saying to Quin, 'I've put out some snacks and drinks, dinner is in the fridge, and there are enough supplies to last a month.'

'Thanks, Fernanda. I appreciate it, as always.'

'No worries, boss—you pay me more than enough to make it worth my while!' She winked at Sadie, then addressed Quin again. 'Elena will come over at some stage to talk through some changes she wants to make to the garden.'

'Okay.'

Sadie turned to Quin. 'How much land is there?'

'About an acre.'

'Wow.'

Sol appeared in the room. 'Come on, Sadie. I want to show you everything.'

She did as she was bade and let Sol take her by the hand and show her around the house, almost thankful for his distracting chatter when a slew of memories rushed back at her on seeing the familiar rooms and then the new ones.

Downstairs, the house had been opened out into a huge living/dining area, and there was a beautiful kitchen overlooking the verdant back lawn where Sadie could see a pool. She noted that Sol was now in what had been her and Quin's bedroom upstairs. She was glad he didn't want to linger there too long. It was too full of memories. The master bedroom suite was now in the dormer extension. There was a balcony, with stunning views of the beach and the sea.

Tears pricked Sadie's eyes as she remembered being on that beach and looking back at this house, catching her first glimpse of Quin on the porch.

'And your room is over here.'

Sadie turned around to see Sol trying to haul her wheelie suitcase into a bedroom across the hall from Quin's. It was almost a mirror image of Quin's, but with no balcony—just windows overlooking the pool and beautiful gardens.

Sadie followed Sol into the room, and to her surprise he ran over and wrapped his arms around her waist. She hugged him back, bending down and pressing a kiss to his head.

He looked up at her. 'I'm glad you're my mom. I knew you were special when I first saw you.'

Sadie's heart swelled at his sweet words. She smiled. 'The minute I saw you, I knew *you* were very special.'

His eyes widened. 'When I was a baby?'

She nodded. 'When you were born, you didn't even cry. You just looked up at me and it was as if you'd been here before—do you know what they call that?'

He shook his head, fascinated. 'No, what?'

'An old soul.'

'Wow, cool.'

And then, like most children, Sol was already moving on, pulling away.

'Come on! Let's find Papa and go to the beach!'

'I'll follow you down.'

But Sol was gone.

Sadie took in a big shuddery breath.

'Okay?'

She whirled around at the sound of Quin's voice. He was wearing jeans and a T-shirt. Relaxed. Sexy. At home here.

She forced her mind away from all Quin's attributes and nodded. 'Fine… You've done an amazing job on the renovations.'

'They were your suggestions, remember?'

Sadie nodded slowly. Yes. She remembered it now. A conversation when she'd listed all the things she'd do if she owned the beach house. She'd been the one who'd said that she'd love a dormer room with a balcony, so she could sit and watch the dawn breaking. Her favourite time of day.

Maybe that was why she hadn't remembered at first— because it was so utterly bittersweet to see that Quin had gone ahead and done it. *Ready for someone else?* Because sooner or later he would move on, and be with another woman. Perhaps marry her. Have more children—siblings for Sol. And where would Sadie fit into that equation? The thought of being further and further sidelined as his new family formed made her feel a sharp pain in her chest.

She realised Quin had walked into his own room and was standing on the balcony. She joined him, still feeling emotional.

Sol's and Fernanda's voices floated up from downstairs.

'Why did you buy it, Quin? After what happened, I would've thought you'd never want to see this place again.'

He didn't answer for a long time, and then he spoke almost as if to himself. 'I stayed here for a month afterwards, with Sol. Expecting that you'd just reappear. I thought maybe you'd suffered some sort of post-partum depression or something. I thought if I waited…'

Sadie said nothing—just looked at Quin's profile.

He went on, 'And then… I think I knew. I couldn't feel you any more. Somehow I knew you were far away. But even when I knew I had to leave—because I had to work and I needed support for me and Sol—I just couldn't let the house go.' He made a little huffing sound. 'You see, even then—as angry as I was—I imagined you returning to the house, finding new people living here and not being able to contact me even though you had my phone number. It was irrational, but I kept on paying the rent after we left. And when the lease was due for renewal I found myself offering to buy it.'

He finally looked at Sadie, and she almost recoiled at the bleak pain she saw in his eyes. She knew it instantly. *He had loved her.*

'Even though I hated you for what you had done to us, I couldn't bear the thought that you might come back and find the place taken over,' he said. He shook his head at himself. 'How messed up is that? In the end I decided we'd use it as a holiday home and had it renovated.'

Sadie looked blindly out at the view, tears blurring her vision. She blinked them back. When she spoke her voice was rough. 'I can't keep saying I'm sorry, Quin. Sooner or later you'll have to accept that we can't go back. I did what I did at the time because I was terrified I would bring harm to you and Sol…and your friend Claude has confirmed how real the danger was…'

She looked at him. The enormity of being back here

was dissolving every wall she'd had to build to protect herself in the last four years. She had nowhere to hide.

She could only say, 'But you need to know that I never stopped loving you, Quin. I still love you. The first thing I did when I learned that I could have my life back was come to find you and Sol.'

If Sadie had hoped that Quin's features would melt at hearing those words and he would gather her into his arms, then she'd been a fool. Still some part of her dared to hope...but he was like stone.

And then he shook his head. 'I'm sorry... I can't...'

Sadie's insides curled in on themselves. Ice went into her veins as some sort of self-protection.

Before she could figure out how to respond, how to get out of this conversation with any shred of dignity, Sol appeared in the doorway of the bedroom.

'Come on, guys...hurry up!'

Sadie looked at her son. He was her focus now. The centre of her world.

She moved away from Quin and went back to her room on wooden legs, somehow forcing a brightness she did not feel into her voice. 'Okay, give me two minutes.'

'I never stopped loving you, Quin... I still love you.'

Quin had heard the words, but it was as if they'd hit a glass wall before they could impact him. In spite of knowing that Sadie had never meant to hurt him, or Sol, he still couldn't seem to let go of the cold, hard pain inside him.

All he could think of—especially here and now, in this place—was that awful moment when he'd returned to find the house empty. Sadie gone. And then...as the minutes and hours had passed…mild concern had given way to confusion, building panic. He'd found her note just when he'd been contemplating calling the police.

He'd gone out into the streets to look for her, not understanding what on earth the note could mean. Surely she was joking? Or maybe she was just unwell.

He'd had Sol strapped to his chest as he'd walked for hours. But there'd been no trace of her.

An awful, liquefying panic had settled into his limbs, making him feel weak. Reminding him of how he'd felt when he'd realised his mother had left him. When he'd found no trace of her left in their house because their father had had all her things removed.

He'd had to sit down on a bench. An old woman had been there. She'd looked at Sol and heard him fretting a little, and she'd smiled and said, 'His mama will be needing him back soon.'

He'd told Sadie just now that he'd kept the house and had it renovated in case she returned, but he knew it went deeper than that and he couldn't ignore it. He hadn't been able to let go of it, in spite of what had happened, because this was where he'd been happiest. And somehow that had eclipsed the pain. But it exposed him now. Exposed his weakness. Just like she'd exposed his weakness before. Making him fall for her. Making him vulnerable. Exposing him to pain.

Quin was still standing on his balcony a few minutes later, when he saw Sadie emerge onto the beach below him with Sol. Her hair was pulled up in a ponytail and she was wearing denim cut-off shorts and a singlet, under which he could see a turquoise bikini top. Her feet were bare.

Something inside him cracked. Like this, even with her paler skin and lighter hair, she looked exactly like the Sadie he'd first met. Shy and blushing. And then bolder, more confident. Chattering non-stop about everything and everything. Passionate. *Loving.*

Sadie might still love him, but her words couldn't even make a dent in the solid wall he'd had to build inside himself to weather the pain of her abandonment. Opening himself up to Sadie again emotionally...*no.* The mere notion made Quin's hand grip onto the railing of the balcony, so tight that his knuckles shone white.

He wouldn't survive. And his son needed him.

His future could not be with this woman, even though he knew she had a right to be in Sol's life. That way lay certain pain. Because he would never not be waiting for the day when he would return to find her gone again. And that made a vice squeeze his chest so hard it hurt.

Sadie and Sol were further down the beach now, kicking a ball. Sol stopped suddenly, and turned and looked back. He saw Quin. He raised his hands to his mouth and shouted something, but Quin couldn't hear what he said. He raised his hand to indicate that he would join them.

It had been a mistake to come here—especially with her. The place was too full of ghosts and memories. He hadn't needed love in his life until he'd met Sadie, and he would never forgive her for making him fall for her. Nor would he ever be so weak again.

A sense of desperation filled him. Surely he would be able to find a way to minimise their contact? He would help set her up in her own place. Find her independence. There would have to be a way. And then this constant craving he felt would surely diminish.

He turned from the view and felt a sense of bleakness lodge in his gut. But bleak was good—better than pain.

That night, Quin woke to sounds of moaning…anguish. Assuming it was Sol, he checked on him—but his son was sleeping soundly in his bed, covers kicked aside, legs askew. Quin pulled the sheet back up and went out into the hall, closing the door softly behind him.

Maybe he'd imagined hearing the—

But it came again, and this time he realised it was from Sadie's room. Afraid she'd wake Sol, Quin went to her room and pushed open the door. Her covers were off too. She wore only sleep shorts and a vest top.

She was moving restlessly. He could see that her skin was slick with perspiration and her head was moving back and forth.

She moaned again. 'No…please, no…don't go away… come back…'

The sense of déjà vu was strong. She'd had nightmares when they'd been together.

Quin went over and put his hands on her arms, holding her gently but firmly. But it seemed to make her worse.

She started thrashing and mumbling incoherently. 'Please…don't try to stop me… No… *No!*'

She shouted that last word and, acting on instinct, Quin bent his head and covered her mouth with his to swallow her cries. He could feel it when her body relaxed under his hands…under his chest.

He pulled back. She was looking at him, eyes wide.

'Quin? Are you…? Am I still dreaming?'

Quin could fee her breasts moving against his chest,

the sharp points of her nipples. He said, 'You were having a nightmare.'

She seemed to look beyond him and said, 'I was... I was on the beach, and you and Sol were really far away, and I was calling you but you couldn't hear me, and you wouldn't turn around, and then someone was holding on to me, stopping me from getting to you...'

Quin felt a shiver down his spine. For a while after Sadie had left he'd had exactly the same dream—except he was the one trying to reach her and she couldn't hear him.

He moved further back, but her hands clasped onto his arms. 'Please, don't leave me yet, Quin.'

Quin gritted his jaw. He'd ignored the temptation to come to her after Sol had fallen asleep earlier; he knew he would never be able to move on if he touched her again. But now his resolve was fast melting into the heat haze clouding his brain and the rising of his blood.

Sadie whispered, 'Can you just stay with me for a bit, please?'

Quin said, 'Move over.'

Sadie scooted into the middle of the bed and Quin lay down behind her, wrapping his arms around her. Holding her. Her backside nestled into his groin, fitting like a missing jigsaw piece. His body responded to her proximity at once, but he exerted every ounce of control to keep it at bay.

Eventually he could feel Sadie relaxing against him, her breaths evening out. He told himself he'd move soon...once he was sure that she was asleep. But, frankly, it felt so familiar and good to hold her like this that he

gave in to the impulse and let his own muscles relax...
until he too found himself drifting off.

Quin was gone when Sadie woke the next morning. But
her body was still humming in the aftermath of what
had happened when they'd both woken in the night to
find themselves entwined. They'd moved to turn face to
face. Sadie had pressed a kiss to Quin's mouth—a *thank
you* for comforting her as much as anything else. She'd
craved his touch so much after that awful dream...she'd
felt so cold.

When she'd kissed him, she'd half expected him to
pull away—because it had been clear he'd had no intention of staying earlier in the night, until she'd begged
him. But after a long moment he'd kissed her back, and
a slow but intense frenzy had overtaken them as they'd
mutually combusted.

She'd told him she loved him.

She waited for a sense of regret and embarrassment,
but it didn't come. She felt lighter. There was no way
she could have kept those words inside—not here in this
place where they'd been so happy. Where they'd made
their beautiful son.

She knew she faced certain heartache now, but it
would be nothing compared to the agony she'd endured
for four years.

Birds tweeted outside. Sadie could hear Sol's voice
downstairs, and she revelled in a brief moment of appreciating where she was, in spite of the realisation that
since they'd arrived here whatever accord she'd reached
with Quin had taken about four steps back.

She got up and showered in the generous en suite

bathroom and dressed in a pair of indigo blue shorts and a matching sleeveless shirt. Sara had packed her bag in Sao Paulo before they'd come here, and it was still such a revelation to be wearing clothes that weren't falling apart at the seams from over-washing.

Tying her hair back roughly, Sadie went downstairs to find Sol seated at the dining table, with his mouth full and a delicious smell of…

'Is that pancakes?'

Sol swallowed his mouthful with comic facial expressions and said, 'Papa made them—they're amazing.'

Quin was behind the kitchen island in a T-shirt, avoiding direct eye contact with Sadie. Her face grew hot just remembering the previous night…

Sol addressed his father. 'Papa, can Mom have pancakes too?'

Sadie's heart stopped and Quin's hands stopped. Now he looked at her, but she couldn't read his expression. She looked at her son, who had no idea what he'd just done by calling her *Mom* for the first time.

Sol looked from her undoubtedly shocked face to Quin. 'What's wrong?'

Quin recovered first, saying briskly, 'Of course she can—and you can have one more and then you need to change for the match.'

A lock of Sol's hair fell forward and he pushed it back. 'Stupid hair… It's getting in my eyes, Papa.'

'You need a trim. We can find a barber shop here later on.'

'I can cut his hair,' Sadie offered, without thinking. She'd used to cut kids' hair all the time.

Sol's eyes bugged. 'You can cut hair?'

Sadie nodded. 'I'm a hairdresser...among other things.'

Jill of all trades... She'd had to be to blend into different places.

'Wow! Papa, did you hear that? She can cut my hair. That's so cool!'

Quin was looking at her. 'Are you sure?'

Sadie shrugged. 'Of course. We can do it after breakfast if there's time. It won't take long.'

'Yes, please. Papa! Can I? Then my hair won't get in the way when I'm playing football.'

Quin shrugged too. 'Sure.'

They had breakfast, Quin serving up more fluffy, light pancakes with fruit and syrup...fragrant coffee. But it was as if last night hadn't happened. For her own sanity Sadie knew she needed to talk to him about it, and what she'd said yesterday, to see if there was any hope at all for them. For a future.

She had to know, because she needed to be able to move on and carve out an existence for herself if Quin really didn't see her in his future.

She took Sol up to the bathroom after breakfast and sat him in a chair, with a towel around his shoulders. Luckily she'd got used to carrying her hairdresser's kit with her, because it was always an easy means to make money.

Sol was looking at her in the mirror with wide eyes, as if fascinated by this creature who was also his mother. She gave him the smallest of buzz cuts around his ears, and then trimmed and styled his hair into a baby Mohican, like the one she'd seen on his favourite football player.

Sol looked at himself. 'I can't wait to show Joao!'

Sadie took off the towel and shook it out over the bath,

and then Sol threw his arms around her waist and buried his head in her belly.

He looked up. 'You're so cool, Mom.'

Sadie said carefully, 'You don't have to call me Mom yet, if it feels weird.'

He shook his head. 'I waited for you for a long time.'

Sadie's heart split open at this unwittingly poignant assessment, but before she could respond Sol was gone again, saying, 'I have to get changed for the match.'

Sadie sat down on the chair she'd used to cut Sol's hair. She had to force herself to remember that it had only been a couple of weeks since she'd come back into Quin's and Sol's lives. Surely this sensation of being on a rollercoaster wouldn't last for ever?

She could hear Quin shouting up the stairs. 'Come on, Sol. Joao will be wondering where you are.'

'I'm coming!'

Even that banal domestic exchange was enough to send her insides swooping with emotion again.

When she'd cleaned up, and felt a bit more together, she went downstairs to find Quin tidying up. Sol had obviously gone to get his friend.

He glanced up. 'Thank you for cutting his hair. He loves it.'

Sadie felt self-conscious. 'Kids that age love a buzz cut.' She could feel the tension in the air and blurted out, 'Look, about last night—'

Quin cut her off. 'I shouldn't have let it happen.' He put down a plate and looked at her. 'I think the shock of seeing you again, and the fact that the chemistry is still there, has blurred the boundaries... But it's not fair on you, me or Sol. He'll get confused if he senses that we're…together.'

Now Sadie felt guilty.

But Quin said, 'It's not your fault.'

The unspoken words were very clear. He was blaming himself for being weak.

'I was the one who had the nightmare. I asked you to stay.'

Begged. Her face grew hot.

A muscle in his jaw popped. 'I could have controlled myself better. I think it was a mistake coming here… I'm not sure if it's a good idea to stay. You've been established now as Sol's mother, so there's no real need to keep up any pretence that we're together.'

Sadie went cold all over. 'If this is because I told you I loved you… Don't ruin your holiday because of me. I can go back to Sao Paulo.'

He looked at her, and then he said, 'That might be for the best. We need to put down some new boundaries. I can arrange transport.'

Sadie's insides were plummeting into a deep void of pain. So this was it. The briefest of fraught honeymoons was over. She chastised herself. She'd known that they needed to talk about this. She just hadn't been prepared for Quin's brutally rapid response and rejection.

'No,' she said, feeling sick. 'I can go to the bus station and get the bus.'

His gaze narrowed on her. 'Is that what you did that day?'

Sadie's gut churned. 'Yes.' And then, before the past could reach out its tentacles to poison the present even more, she asked, 'Is there no chance at all of us trying... to be a family?'

An expression somewhere between anger and pain flashed across Quin's face. 'I grieved for you, Sadie,' he said roughly. 'I've never grieved for anyone in my life—not even my own mother. But I grieved for you. And I won't ever risk that kind of hurt or loss again.'

Sadie's heart ached. 'I love you, Quin, and I never want you to be hurt again. I never wanted to hurt you in the first place. You gave me the only sense of belonging and home that I've ever had. *You* are my home. You are my world. You are everything that I love and adore, and I will never, ever leave you and Sol again if you give me a chance.'

Sadie stopped talking. She was raw.

Quin just looked at her, and she could see the pain in his eyes. The pain she had put there. The pain she feared was insurmountable.

And he confirmed it when he shook his head. 'No, I can't do it, Sadie.'

She couldn't breathe. And then, in the distance, she heard Sol's excited voice, and suddenly knew she wouldn't be able to keep it together if he saw her.

So she said, 'I'll go upstairs and start packing. Just tell Sol I had to go back early.'

Quin nodded. 'I'll be gone for the day too.'

So this was it.

Sadie looked at Quin, feeling as if her heart was being ripped out of her chest, still beating. It was agony, being sent away like this, but she couldn't argue with him. Sol had to come first, and if there was any danger of him getting too attached, and then confused by their actions, Sadie would never forgive herself.

The last four years had strengthened her in ways that she was only appreciating now. She could do this. She had no choice.

'Goodbye, Quin.'

His face was like stone. 'We'll discuss what happens next back in Sao Paulo.'

CHAPTER TWELVE

QUIN'S VERY BRITTLE sense of satisfaction lasted until about half-time in the football game—not that he'd been able to focus on it up to that point. All he could see in his mind's eye was the pale set to Sadie's face and the pleading look in her eyes for his understanding when she'd disappeared before Sol returned.

And then the look of abject disappointment on Sol's face when she hadn't been there.

Quin had felt like the lowest of the low, knowing he was hurting his son, but if anything Sol's disappointment only proved that he was doing the right thing in setting down boundaries.

He pictured her now, getting on the bus to Sao Paulo, repeating the journey she'd taken that fateful day four years ago.

And suddenly the flimsy, brittle facade of control he'd been clinging on to fell apart like shards of glass falling out of a window frame, cutting him so deep that he realised this was the first time he'd felt such pain in four years.

The kind of pain he'd thought he'd avoid because he was in control here.

Hadn't he'd just demonstrated that by sending Sadie

away? Before she could leave again and rip his heart out and tear it to pieces.

But it hadn't worked. Because he was no more in control of his pain now than he'd been in control of anything since he'd laid eyes on her again and his life had been spun off its axis—much like the way it had when he'd first laid eyes on her.

She'd told him she loved him. That she'd never stopped. Her words had been lying in wait inside him and were now detonating like bombs, intensifying that pain, mocking him for believing that he was impenetrable.

Quin felt as if he was unravelling at the seams. Cracking open. Losing his bearings. Everything he'd clung to for the past four years was dissolving and being replaced with a vast abyss, into which he was falling with nothing to grab on to.

Suddenly he knew what he had to do. He felt wild, desperate. Urgent.

It was half-time. Sol was there in front of him. 'Did you see the goal I nearly got? I wish Mom was here— maybe then I would have scored.'

Quin knelt down on one knee. He said, 'There's something I need to go and do, so I'm going to arrange for you to go home with Joao afterwards. Is that okay?'

Looking wise beyond his years, but also very much like a little boy who had just got his mother back, he said, 'If it's to do with Mom then, yes, that's okay.'

Quin kissed his son and made a phone call. He left the football ground and went straight to the bus station.

But the bus to Sao Paulo had already left.

He felt sick. He'd just put Sadie through the cruelty of repeating the horrific journey she'd made when she'd left them, all because Quin was determined to beat her with the stick of his mother's sins. And his own cowardice.

Enough. It was time to move on.

All he could think of to do now, though, was to go back to the house. He would have time to think while Sol was with his friend.

When he got back to the house he stopped at the door, the pain in his chest intensifying. He knew he was about to walk into an empty house. And this time he couldn't blame Sadie for leaving because he was the one who had engineered this painful re-enactment.

He deserved every ounce of pain he was feeling.

He opened the door and went inside, steeling himself for the house to be empty. And it was. But then Quin noticed that the door leading out to the porch was open, the warm sea breeze making the curtains move.

He frowned. He was sure he'd closed the door, but maybe Sol had run back out to get something just before they'd left.

He went over and stopped on the threshold. Because someone was outside, standing at the railing. *Sadie.* Here. Not gone. Was he hallucinating? Conjuring her up? Like he had so many times in the past? Like in the dreams he'd had?

She turned around and saw him. Her eyes were huge and suspiciously red. She shook her head and said brokenly, 'I'm so sorry, but I just…couldn't get on the bus. I couldn't do it, Quin. I couldn't take that journey again… away from here, away from you and Sol.'

Quin closed his eyes for a second and sent up a silent promise to every deity that he would spend his lifetime atoning for this if he was lucky enough to get the chance.

He moved forward and touched Sadie. She was real.

He pulled her into his arms and said, 'I'm so sorry for doing that to you…please forgive me.'

Sadie revelled in the way Quin was holding her for a long moment, not daring to breathe in case this was a cruel mirage and he disappeared. But he felt so solid, and his heart was beating so steadily. Maybe a tiny bit fast.

She knew she should pull away before she dared to hope…*anything*. But Quin was the one to put his hands on her arms and put some distance between them. She couldn't look at him. She was sure she must be a sight. She hadn't stopped crying since she'd let the bus go, anticipating Quin's anger that she was still here. But he didn't seem angry.

He tipped up her chin and she had to look at him. There was an expression on his face that she hadn't seen since they'd met again. *Open*. Contrite.

He said, 'I need to say some things, okay?'

Sadie just nodded. Quin led her over to one of the recliner chairs and gently pushed her down. She welcomed it; her legs were like jelly. He stayed standing, then he moved away and stood with his back to the railing and the view.

He looked at her and said, 'When my mother left, I blamed myself.'

Sadie wanted to go to him, but she was aware of the fragility of this moment. 'You were only a toddler.'

'Yes, I was only a baby. But I remember holding on to her, begging her not to go. Crying. Afterwards I thought it was my fault because I'd been too emotional, too overwrought, so after that it became habitual for me to ignore my emotions and to compartmentalise things.'

'And then you came along,' he went on, 'and with one look at you, before we'd even spoken, I felt every single wall I'd built up inside me to keep me safe start crumbling to pieces.'

Sadie felt shy. 'I was a nobody…'

Quin shook his head. 'No. You were amazing.'

Hope sparked inside Sadie, but she tried not to let it bloom. 'But then I lost my memory… I didn't even know who I was.'

Quin's mouth tipped up. 'You were probably more authentically you precisely *because* you had no memory of who you were. You weren't like any woman I'd ever met. There was no artifice. No games. Everything you felt showed on your face. You found joy in everything. It was so obvious that you loved me—'

'Stop!' Sadie ducked her head, letting her hair fall down.

But Quin came over and sat down near her. He took her hands and made sure she was looking at him before he said, 'I couldn't help falling fathoms deep in love with you. It would have taken a force stronger than I was capable of to resist you.'

Sadie bit her lip and then said, 'I wasn't sure if you ever *had* loved me.'

Quin's gaze was on her mouth, then it moved up to her eyes. 'More than I'd loved anyone else in my life. I hadn't truly loved before, and it was only when you left that I realised how much you'd changed me. It compounded my feeling of betrayal. I felt so naked…exposed.'

Sadie tensed. Nothing had changed. She pulled back from his hands. 'I can't keep apologising, Quin—

But he stopped her words as he reached for her and covered her mouth with his. Surprise and shock made her go still.

He pulled back. 'I don't want you to apologise ever again. You have nothing to be sorry for. It's only now that I'm a father that I can appreciate the selfless bravery it took for you to do what you did. And you shame me—because I'm not sure if I could have done it.'

Sadie was confused. 'Quin…what?'

'If anyone owes apologies, it's me.'

'But you didn't do anything.'

Quin let out a short, harsh sound and stood up from the seat. He went back to the porch railing. Sadie got up too and went to stand beside him. He wouldn't look at her.

'I let you clean my house, Sadie…'

'I offered to clean. I wanted to feel useful.'

He looked at her and she saw the shame in his eyes.

'You offered to clean because I made you feel like an unwanted guest.'

'You were shocked to see me.'

Quin let out another harsh sound, half a laugh and half something else. Anguish. 'Why did you let me treat you like that?'

'Because I was finally back with you and my son. And, frankly, cleaning a bathroom was nothing compared to what I'd endured for four years. I was willing to do anything to absolve the horrible guilt I felt.'

Quin took her by the hand again and led her over to the recliner, sitting down and pulling her onto his lap, wrapping his arms around her. Sadie knew something momentous was happening, but she was too afraid to call it what it was. It didn't necessarily mean what she hoped it meant.

Nevertheless, she let herself melt into him, his strong, powerful body holding hers. She felt the ever-present hum of desire between them, but she also felt something infinitely deeper that transcended desire. After a long moment he spoke, and she could feel his chest rumbling under her cheek.

'The whole time I told myself I was hating you, I still loved you. The whole time I told myself I should never have trusted you, I was really angry for trusting myself— for letting myself fall so hard for a woman who would cruelly re-enact the worst betrayal I'd ever experienced.'

Sadie opened her mouth—but, as if reading her mind, Quin put a finger to her lips.

'I have to say this,' he said. 'That was just a tragic co-incidence, but I clung to it for four years, because hating you and blaming you was easier than admitting how much I loved you and how hurt I was. It helped me survive, I'm ashamed to say.'

Sadie tipped her head back and looked up at him. 'I'm sure I would have done the same.'

Quin looked down at her and shook his head. 'No way. You weren't cynical, like me. I'd forgotten how cynical I was—I thought that was your fault too. Believe me, anything I could have blamed you for I latched on to it like a drowning man to a buoy in the middle of the ocean.'

'If it helped you survive, then I don't mind.'

Quin's fingers traced her jaw and his mouth quirked. 'No, you wouldn't. Because you're a far better person than me, Sadie Ryan.'

Sadie's heart hitched. She came up higher and rested her hand on Quin's chest. The way he was holding her… the things he was saying…she was too afraid to let this go further if his endgame was still to send her away.

'What are you saying? Do you still want me to leave?'

His jaw tightened, and then he said, 'Have you not noticed that since the moment you appeared in front of me in New York I pretty much haven't let you out of my sight? And that we were in bed again within days?'

'Yes…but—'

'And that when I do send you away I last for approximately three hours before my world implodes and I have to get you back? I went to the bus station and the bus had gone…' He shook his head. 'I'll never forgive myself for making you do that.'

Sadie caught his hand and kissed it. 'But I didn't go. I'm here.'

Quin's eyes looked suspiciously bright. 'That's because you're brave and loving and kind and—'

She stopped his words with her mouth, and when she pulled back she said, 'I was too scared to get on the bus—afraid that if I did, something would happen and I'd never see you again…or Sol.'

Quin pulled her close again. 'Thank God for that.' He cupped her jaw. 'And you are an amazing mother—you protected him, and me, by risking your own life.' A shudder went through his body and he said, 'Jesus, Sadie, if anything had happened to you…'

She put her hands on his chest. 'It didn't. And the danger is gone. We're free now.'

Quin took one of her hands and held it to him. With

emotion thick in his throat he said, 'I love you, Sadie… can you forgive me?'

The emotion she'd been so carefully holding back threatened to burst like a dam. 'Forgive you for what?'

'For being so hard on you…for asking you to leave…'

Tears pricked Sadie's eyes. 'Forgiven, my love.'

He smiled. 'Say that again.'

Sadie smiled too, and it was wobbly. 'Which bit?'

His eyes flashed. 'You know.'

She kissed him and then pulled back. 'My love…'

'I love you too—so much. And if you'll let me I want to spend the rest of my life showing you how much.'

Quin lowered his head to hers, sealing his words with a kiss that was so tender, and so full of all the longing Sadie had lived with for four years, that emotion ran over and leaked out of her eyes.

When they stopped kissing, Quin wiped her tears away. He said, 'No more tears, okay?'

Sadie half chuckled. 'I'll try my best.'

They sat in harmonious silence for a long time, watching the afternoon turn into evening and dusk. Eventually Sadie asked where Sol was, and Quin told her he was sleeping over at his friend's.

He stood up and held out his hand. She put her hand into his and let him lead her up to the bedroom as the dusk disappeared into the moonlight outside and the waves lapped against the shore.

They made love and talked and drifted into a doze, before making love again and finally falling into sleep.

When Quin woke he looked up and saw Sadie standing on the balcony with a sheet around her, watching the sunrise. He got up and went over to her, naked, and she leant back into his embrace. For the first time in four years he felt whole again. At peace.

She looked up at him and smiled. 'Come for a walk?'

He nodded. 'Anywhere, any time.'

They'd used to say that to each other. She'd stop him working on his laptop and say, *'Come for a walk?'* and he would take one look at her and say, *'Anywhere...any time.'*

They showered and got dressed and then walked along the shore, hand in hand, close together, not even speaking, just letting the moment wash over them and through them, healing all the pain and loss that they'd endured for four years.

They walked all the way to the end and then started back. Other people were on the beach now, jogging or walking their dogs before the heat of the day set in. There were some early surfers.

About halfway back, Sadie stopped. 'This is where we got married.'

Quin looked to the spot where she was pointing. 'How do you know?'

'Because it was the best day of my life, and thinking about it sustained me every day for the last four years. I can remember Sol kicking in my belly as we were making our vows.'

Quin turned to face her, pulling her close. He smiled. 'I remember him kicking too...and I remember how we celebrated.'

Sadie blushed and buried her head in Quin's chest. He smiled at the memory. She'd been very...amorous in her pregnancy.

He lifted her chin with his finger and she looked up at him. Such joy filled him that it almost scared him with its intensity. Had last night really happened?

As if reading his mind, Sadie whispered, 'I'm afraid this isn't real. That this is just a dream.'

Quin pushed the doubts and fears away. *No more.* 'It's real. We're here, together again. Please reassure me that no matter what happens in the future we'll deal with it together, as a team.'

Sadie smiled. 'I promise.'

'And will you marry me? Officially?' The words flowed out of Quin's mouth.

Sadie didn't skip a beat. 'Of course.'

'How about we go and get our son and have breakfast, and then start living the rest of our lives together?'

Sadie's eyes were suspiciously bright. 'I'd really like that.'

So they went to get their son—who squealed when he saw Sadie and ran straight into her arms. They held a hand each as they walked back to their beach house while Sol chattered happily. They looked at each other over his head and smiled, and then they did start living their lives again…together for ever, in love and at peace.

EPILOGUE

Three years and nine months later, Sao Sebastiao

'THERE ARE TOO many women in this family,' Sol grumbled good-naturedly as he moved his younger charges away from the danger of the open gate that led onto the beach, taking care to close it behind him. He really adored his three-year-old twin sisters, Luna and Stella, but he'd never let on—because at the grand age of nearly eight he was far too grown up to be mushy.

The girls were non-identical, their colouring closer to Quin's than to Sadie's this time. Dark eyes full of mischief.

Quin's voice was close to Sadie's ear. 'Do you think we should put him out of his misery and tell him he'll soon have a baby brother?'

He patted Sadie's sizeable bump under her one-piece swimsuit. She was lying with her back to his chest, his long legs spread out each side of her.

She squeezed a firm, muscular thigh and chuckled. 'No harm in letting him appreciate his outnumbering by women for a little longer.'

They'd been officially married in Sao Paulo, with Sol

as their very proud ring-bearer, not long after that first trip back to the beach house.

In spite of her protestations that she didn't need one, Sadie now had a wedding band that was the perfect accompaniment to her first wedding ring, inlaid with diamonds, emeralds and sapphires.

She'd almost forgotten the pain of their four years of forced estrangement. Only very rarely now did she have a bad dream, and Quin was always there to wake her, and remind her that she was safe and loved and at home.

At home. With her family. Safe and loved.

They were literally creating a life full of love and happiness, giving their children all the things they hadn't had, and not for one second did they take it for granted.

Sol stomped up the steps to where they were sitting on their beloved porch and sighed dramatically before saying, 'I think we need to take the girls for a walk on the beach. Or they'll never go down for their afternoon nap and I will have no peace.'

Sadie could feel the effort it took for Quin not to laugh out loud as he gently disentangled himself from her. She sat up with a *huff,* feeling more and more like a beached whale every day.

He pulled her up from the seat and they donned hats and more suncream and set off to the beach—just one family among all the others, no more remarkable than anyone else. Except they *were*—because of the trials they'd endured and survived. And because of their rare love.

Quin wrapped an arm around Sadie's waist and they followed in the wake of Sol and his little sisters, who trotted devotedly in his wake on their sturdy little legs.

'Happy?' Quin asked, looking down at Sadie.

She looked up and grinned. 'So happy.'

A few weeks later Kai was born, and their love and happiness was multiplied. But, much more importantly, Sol was no longer outnumbered by women.

* * * * *

Did you fall in love with The Heir Dilemma?
*Then don't miss out on these other fabulous stories
from Abby Green!*

His Housekeeper's Twin Baby Confession
Mistaken as His Royal Bride
Claimed by the Crown Prince
Heir for His Empire
"I Do" For Revenge

Available now!